Noise erupted in the room.

Gasps. Shouts. Even a scream. But she could barely hear them for the blood rushing through her head, roaring in her ears. Her pulse pounded madly with adrenaline and attraction. Had it been so long since she'd been kissed that any man could affect her like this? It couldn't be just because it was Logan. She couldn't want a man that she hated as much as this one.

No man had ever kissed her the way he was kissing her—with so much passion and desire that her knees weakened and her head swam and she completely forgot why she'd kissed him in the first place.

When he pulled back, she was panting for breath, and her heart was beating so quickly that it pounded against her breasts. Against her lips, he murmured, "What the hell are you up to?"

For a moment she couldn't remember. Then it came back to her: the plan—his mother's outrageous plan.

She whispered back, "I'm saving your life." Then she turned toward her stunned family and announced, "Logan Payne is my fiancé. We're getting married."

EXPLOSIVE ENGAGEMENT

—

LISA CHILDS

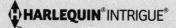

HARLEQUIN® INTRIGUE®

For my family—with great appreciation for all your love and support. Love you all!

Recycling programs for this product may not exist in your area.

ISBN-13: 978-0-373-74827-3

EXPLOSIVE ENGAGEMENT

Copyright © 2014 by Lisa Childs

All rights reserved. Except for use in any review, the reproduction or utilization of this work in whole or in part in any form by any electronic, mechanical or other means, now known or hereafter invented, including xerography, photocopying and recording, or in any information storage or retrieval system, is forbidden without the written permission of the publisher, Harlequin Enterprises Limited, 225 Duncan Mill Road, Don Mills, Ontario M3B 3K9, Canada.

This is a work of fiction. Names, characters, places and incidents are either the product of the author's imagination or are used fictitiously, and any resemblance to actual persons, living or dead, business establishments, events or locales is entirely coincidental.

This edition published by arrangement with Harlequin Books S.A.

For questions and comments about the quality of this book, please contact us at CustomerService@Harlequin.com.

® and TM are trademarks of Harlequin Enterprises Limited or its corporate affiliates. Trademarks indicated with ® are registered in the United States Patent and Trademark Office, the Canadian Intellectual Property Office and in other countries.

Printed in U.S.A.

ABOUT THE AUTHOR

Bestselling, award-winning author Lisa Childs writes paranormal and contemporary romance for Harlequin. She lives on thirty acres in Michigan with her two daughters, a talkative Siamese and a long-haired Chihuahua who thinks she's a rottweiler. Lisa loves hearing from readers, who can contact her through her website, www.lisachilds.com, or snail-mail address, P.O. Box 139, Marne, MI 49435.

Books by Lisa Childs

CAST OF CHARACTERS

Logan Payne—The former detective and CEO of Payne Protection needs a bodyguard himself after attempts on his life. Instead he winds up with a fiancée.

Stacy Kozminski—She has hated Logan Payne for keeping her father in prison, so he's the last man she would marry—until murder attempts leave her no other option but to propose.

Patek Kozminski—The former jewel thief took his secrets to his grave, but someone thinks he may have shared them with his daughter—which puts her in danger.

Garek Kozminski—Stacy's brother has done prison time, and he's not above breaking the law again...this time for revenge.

Milek Kozminski—Stacy's other brother has also had scrapes with the law. Like Garek, he'll do anything to protect their sister—even kill....

Iwan Kozminski—Uncle Iwan was Patek's partner in the jewel thefts, but he never went to prison...and he'll do anything to make sure he never does.

Marta Kozminski—She enjoys the lifestyle her husband Iwan provides, and she's not going to let his brother's children and Logan Payne mess that up.

Candace Baker—The bodyguard is so in love with her boss that she would give her life for his. She might also take a life—that of his fiancée.

Robert Cooper—The retired police officer was Logan's dad's partner and the key witness in Patek Kozminski's trial, which puts him in danger too.

Parker Payne—Being Logan's twin has already put him in danger, but he would gladly take a bullet for his brother.

Nikki Payne—The baby and only Payne sister, Nikki is determined to prove she's just as tough as her brothers.

Penny Payne—The Payne family matriarch is not part of her children's security business. As a wedding planner, she believes in another kind of security—happily ever after—and she's not above taking advantage of a situation to ensure her kids are happy.

Prologue

The bomb was set, so he carefully closed the door. When it opened again, the timer would activate—giving the victim mere minutes before the explosion. He exited the back door and breathed a sigh of relief that he was out of danger.

No. He wasn't out of danger yet—not until the bomb claimed its intended victim. He didn't enjoy killing, but he'd done it—more than once—out of necessity. He'd had to do it to protect himself.

That was all he was doing now—making sure that no one was left alive to link him to his crimes. Then, after all these years, he might finally have peace.

Chapter One

The sun shone brightly, setting the white bricks of the church aglow. It was a great day for a wedding. But Logan Payne couldn't forget that a funeral was also taking place today. He'd thought it might finally bring him some peace that his father's killer was dead. But it seemed more like an injustice that the man had lived for only fifteen years of his already too short sentence.

Maybe it was that sense of injustice that had made Logan uneasy. Or maybe it was the recent attempts on his life.

But he pushed aside that uneasiness and focused instead on the bride and groom. He lifted his hand, with birdseed stuck to his palm, and waved off his younger brother and his new bride. Nobody deserved happiness more than the two of them—especially after the hell they had endured to be together.

His sister, Nikki, glanced up at him through the tears glistening in her warm brown eyes. "Getting emotional, big bro?" she teased. Their family relentlessly teased each other.

The tears were all hers, but he played along. "Birdseed got in my eye," he said with an exaggerated blink. But then he squinted at a random glare and glanced toward the street where his brother's decorated SUV sat on the curb. Nikki had written Just Married across the back window and tied strings of pop cans to the rear bumper. A car slowly passed it, and as it did, a barrel protruded out of the dark tinted driver's window.

The SUV shielded the bride and groom, but Logan and his sister and his twin were exposed on the steps of the church. As the shots rang out, he knocked Nikki down and lunged at Parker, knocking him over the railing.

The shots weren't meant for any of his siblings. He knew that. But he had been standing too close to Nikki. And his twin was identical—same black hair, same blue eyes, same features. Today they were even both wearing black tuxedos. Logan covered Nikki's petite frame, shielding her with his body. And he tensed, waiting for the bullets to find their target in his flesh.

Tires squealed as the car rounded the corner and drove off. After a glance over his shoulder to make certain the shooter was gone, Logan helped his sister to her feet. She trembled with fear in his arms, but she was unhurt. Miraculously, Logan hadn't been hit, either.

The bride, Tanya, turned away from the SUV and ran back to the church. The groom, Cooper, was right beside her, yelling the name of his missing brother. "Parker!"

A hand rose above the shrubs on the side of the church's wide front steps. Cooper clasped it and pulled Parker from the branches and foliage.

"You okay?" Cooper asked him.

"Yeah, yeah," Parker replied as he brushed off his tux. "Logan knocked me over and pushed down Nikki." He waited—probably for Logan to make some smart-aleck comeback. That was the way the Paynes handled stuff—emotional stuff, dangerous stuff…with gallows humor.

But Logan couldn't find any humor in this situation. The grudge he'd been carrying, and how he'd acted on that grudge, was what had nearly killed his family. And these weren't the first attempts made on his life and Parker's, who must have been mistaken for him then, too.

"I'm sorry," he said.

His new sister-in-law's voice trembled with concern as she said, "I thought it was over. Mr. Gregory is dead."

Logan had been the one who'd taken the shot that had ended the life of her grandfather's lawyer.

The man had been trying to kill her so that no one would discover that he'd embezzled her inheritance.

"This isn't about you," Logan assured the beautiful blonde bride. Guilt twisted his guts into knots. He hated that this shooting—that *his* problem—had marred what had finally been the perfect wedding for Tanya and Cooper. "This is about me. And revenge…"

Cooper's eyes, which were the same blue as his and Parker's, narrowed with suspicion, and he accused him, "You know who it is."

Anger, more intense and overwhelming than his guilt, surged through Logan. He knew who was behind all these cowardly shootings. He knew and he was damn well going to put a stop to it.

For the first time in fifteen years, Stacy Kozminski didn't have to go through prison security to see her father. All she had to do was walk up the aisle of the dimly lit church to where he lay in a casket before the altar. But that walk was the most difficult she had ever taken. Her knees trembled with each step she took, shaking more the closer she got to the altar.

To the casket…

The lid was open, but she needed to take a few more steps to see past the flower arrangements. Her knees shook even harder, threatening to give out beneath her. Maybe she would have crumpled right there, but a strong arm wrapped around her waist in support.

She uttered a sigh of relief that at least one of her brothers had showed up...because she had been the first and only family member to arrive at the church. With a smile on her lips, she turned her head, but the smile froze when her gaze collided with Logan Payne's.

His blue eyes icy hard with anger, he stared down at her.

He was mad at *her?* She was the one who should be angry—furious even because he had no right to show up at her father's funeral at all—let alone wearing a tuxedo. Her heart skipped a beat before the rate sped up. He looked damn good in the black tux with the pleated white shirt. The black bow tie had already been undone and the once-white silk shirt was a little smudged and rumpled. But still...

She hated him; she reminded herself of that as she jerked away from the unsettling warmth of his long, hard body. "What the hell are you doing here?"

And why had he put his arm around her? He was the last person from whom she would ever expect support—especially today.

"I think you know," he replied, his deep voice vibrating with anger.

She shook her head. "I have no idea...unless you want to make sure that he's really dead..."

With a trembling hand, she gestured toward the casket and toppled over one of the flower arrangements. The vase rolled across the tiled floor, leaving a trail of multicolored petals and water behind it. She gasped at what she'd done.

But Logan Payne didn't react. He was staring at the casket. Maybe she had been right about his reason for coming.

She followed his gaze to her father's corpse. She'd already seen it when he'd died. She had made it to the prison in time to say goodbye. Wasn't that supposed to have given her closure?

Stacy felt no calm acceptance. No gratefulness. She felt nothing but anger—all toward Logan Payne. So she turned back to him, and then she turned *on* him. Literally lashing out at him in her anger, she swung her hand toward his unfairly handsome face.

The man had some crazy reflexes, because he caught her wrist, stopping her palm just short of one of his chiseled cheekbones. Despite not slapping him, her skin tingled—maybe with the need to slap him yet. Maybe because he was touching her, his long fingers wrapped easily and tightly around her narrow wrist.

"I can't believe even you are such a heartless bastard that you'd show up at my father's funeral," she said, lashing out now with her words. "And in a tux, no less."

He glanced down at himself, as if he'd forgotten what he was wearing.

"But then I guess this is a celebration for you," she continued. "Do you intend to dance on his grave at the cemetery, too?"

She would make damn sure of it that he never got the chance—even if she had to throw him out herself since no other mourners had arrived yet. Where the hell were her brothers?

They had always been there for her when she needed them most. Until today…

"I've already been dancing," Logan replied.

She struggled against his grasp; she didn't want a man capable of such a hateful comment touching her.

"At my brother's wedding," he continued.

That explained the tux.

"But then somebody tried to kill me," he said. "Again."

That explained his white shirt being smudged and rumpled and his thick black hair disheveled, as if he'd been running his hands through it. What would it feel like? Coarse or soft? Not that she cared to ever find out. She didn't want to touch Logan Payne, and she sure as hell didn't want him touching her.

So she tried again to wriggle free of his hold. "Why are you telling me this?" she asked. "Do you think I care?"

"I think you're behind it," he said.

"Me?" She hadn't even been able to slap him. "How am I supposed to have tried to kill you?"

"You shot at me," he said.

"I don't own a gun." Her brothers had tried to give her one for protection, but she'd refused. Her protection had a threatening growl and a mouthful of sharp teeth to back up his threats. Too bad she hadn't been able to bring Cujo to the funeral.

He snorted derisively, as if he doubted her. Of course he doubted her; Logan Payne doubted *everyone*.

"You're doing it again," she said. "Accusing someone of a crime they didn't commit." She turned back to the casket. Her father was only in his early fifties but he looked much older. Prison had turned his brown hair white and etched deep lines in his tense face. Wasn't he supposed to look peaceful, like he was sleeping? But even in death, her father had found no peace—probably because of Logan Payne.

"I didn't accuse your father," he reminded her. "He was caught at the scene. He was tried and convicted."

"Of murder," she said. Shaking her head yet at the injustice, she added, "My father was not a murderer."

Patek Kozminski had been a lot of things—by his own admission—but he could have never taken a life. The judge and jury had come to the wrong conclusion.

"He killed my father," Logan said with all the rage and anguish as if it had just happened yesterday instead of fifteen years ago.

She shook her head again.

"My father caught him in the commission of a felony…"

Logan Payne was no longer a police officer, but he still talked like one. His father had been a police officer, too, who'd caught her father robbing a jewelry store.

"He resisted arrest," he continued, "they struggled over the gun. And my father wound up dead."

"My father did not kill him." The man she'd known and loved wouldn't have resisted arrest; he wouldn't have fought with a police officer. He wouldn't have wrestled the gun away from him and shot him with it. There had to have been someone else there that horrible day, someone else who'd really committed the crime…

"My father is dead," Logan said.

"And now so is mine," she said, gesturing again to the casket, but this time she was careful not to knock over any flower arrangements. "Are you happy?"

Logan sighed. "No."

"No, of course not," she hotly agreed. "You would have rather he lived many, many more years and spent every one of them behind bars. That's why you showed up at every parole hearing to make sure he didn't get out."

"He killed a man!" Logan said.

Tears stung her eyes, and she shook her head. "No, no, he didn't…" There had to have been someone else…

"The judge and jury convicted him," he said it almost gently now, as if Logan Payne had any concern for her feelings.

He hadn't, or he would have stopped showing up at the parole hearings; he would have let her father get out of prison. If not for Logan fighting it, her father would have been granted parole. He had been a model prisoner.

He had been a model father, too—even from behind bars. Now she had no father at all. She could almost relate to Logan's rage, but hers was directed at him.

"He wasn't convicted of murder, though," he said, correcting her earlier comment. "It was manslaughter."

"Which is why he had been up for parole already four times." And why he would have been released…if not for Logan Payne.

"It should have been murder," he said. "The charge was too light. So was the sentence…"

"The sentence wound up being death," she said. "You gave him that sentence."

"I didn't—"

"If you hadn't showed up at those hearings, he would have been released. He wouldn't have been there for that crazy prisoner to stab. He wouldn't have been behind bars with animals like that!" She swung her other hand now. But his damn reflexes were so fast that he caught her wrist again. She struggled against his grasp and cursed him.

But Logan didn't even blink at her insults. His gaze remained steady and intense on her face. He was always so damn intense. Despite her rising temper, her flesh tingled and chilled, lifting goose bumps on her skin—even skin that was covered by her new black sweater dress.

"What the hell's going on?" a familiar voice demanded to know.

"Get your damn hands off her, Payne!" another voice chimed in.

Her brothers had finally arrived. She'd wanted them earlier—to be there for support over her father's funeral. But now she felt a rush of fear as they ran down the aisle toward her and Logan. She was actually afraid for Logan because her brothers were very protective of her—to the point that they had even killed for her.

Were they about to do that again?

Chapter Two

Logan released her—so abruptly that Stacy stumbled back. He would have reached for her again, just to steady her, but one of her brothers caught her. The other one reached for him. Garek or Milek—he didn't know who was whom. They weren't twins, but they looked nearly as much alike as he and Parker did. These guys were tall, too, but with blond hair and gray eyes.

Stacy had the same smoky-gray eyes—with thick lashes she kept blinking. Not to flirt with him—he was the last man she'd ever flirt with—but to fight back tears over her father's death. Her hair wasn't as blond as her brothers. It had streaks of brown and bronze and gold.

He jerked away from whichever brother was grabbing at him. Then he dodged the fist the man swung, even more easily than he had dodged Stacy's attempts to slap him. Maybe he should have just let her hit him. Maybe then she would have gotten the revenge she sought.

No. He doubted her quest for revenge would be satisfied until he was as dead as their fathers.

She might have been telling the truth about not owning a gun. But she didn't need to; she had brothers who would do anything she told them and that was the same as pulling the trigger.

He reached beneath the tuxedo jacket for *his* gun.

"Really?" Stacy asked, her voice shaking with anger. "You're going to pull a gun at my father's funeral?"

He paused with his hand on his holster. "Would you rather I just let them kill me?" He mentally smacked himself for the dumb comment. Of course she would rather he just let them. That was the whole point of trying to murder him.

"They're not going to kill you."

"Don't lie to him, Stace," one of them said.

"You're not going to kill him," she said with a meaningful glare at both of her brothers. "We are not going to ruin our father's funeral."

And that was the only reason that she wouldn't let them kill him *here*—in the dark church with its dingy stained-glass windows and scratched up tile floor. It wasn't as pretty and bright as the church he'd just left—the one his mother had bought and turned into a wedding chapel and reception hall.

"You don't think he's ruining it," one of the brothers asked, "by showing up here in a freaking tuxedo?"

Regret flashed through Logan, but he'd been so damn angry—and with damn good reason—that he hadn't considered how he was dressed before he'd rushed over from one church to another. "Sorry, I didn't have a chance to change between my brother's wedding and getting shot at."

"*If* you were shot at during your brother's wedding, maybe it had something to do with him or his bride," she said. "Why do you automatically assume it had anything to do with me or my family?"

"Because it did," he said with total certainty.

She shook her head. "We can't be the only enemies you've ever made."

Probably not, but he wasn't about to admit that to *her.* "Usually people appreciate what I do for them."

"You expect us to *appreciate* you keeping our father in prison?" she asked, her gray eyes widening with shock and outrage.

"Let me kill him," one of the brothers pleaded with her.

She was younger than them, but she was definitely the one calling the shots, literally, in the Kozminski family. She stared at her father's body lying in the bronze casket and shook her head. "Not here, Garek."

Not "no," just "not here."

"And you wonder why I think it's you behind the attempts on my life…"

"Attempts?" she repeated.

The one she'd called Garek laughed. "And there's your proof that it's not us," he said. "We wouldn't have had to try more than once to kill you."

"I own a security firm," he reminded them. "I will not be easy to kill."

"I don't know..." the other brother, Milek, mused as he walked around Logan. "You showed up here alone."

"He's not alone," a deep voice very much like his own announced from the back of the church.

Of course Parker would have figured out where he'd gone. But he hadn't come alone, either. Their little sister had tagged along like she always had when they were kids. She hadn't outgrown that annoying habit yet. Fortunately, one of Payne Protection Agency's most loyal employees had come along, too. Candace Baker stood next to Parker, her hand beneath her jacket, probably on her holster.

Instead of being grateful for the backup, Logan was incredibly annoyed with the interference. And the doubt. He could take care of himself and them, and he had proven that again and again.

"What the hell are all of you doing here?" he demanded to know.

"Mom sent us," his twin replied.

"Of course she did." Their mother had a problem remembering that *he* ran Payne Protection—not her. Logan had overlooked her interference when it had involved her matchmaking his brother with his new bride. But he didn't want her interfering in his life. "She had no right…"

"That didn't stop *you*," Stacy bitterly remarked.

"I had no right to what, dear?" Penny Payne asked as she joined them in the church. Unlike him and Parker who wore the wedding tuxedos, she'd changed from her bronze-colored mother-of-the-bride gown into a black dress. She hadn't been on the steps to see off Cooper and Tanya. She must have been changing then—as if she'd always intended to attend the funeral of the man who'd murdered her husband.

"Why are you here, Mom?" he asked. He doubted he would ever understand her, but neither had his father. It hadn't stopped Nicholas Payne from loving her, though. And it wouldn't stop Logan, either, unless he wound up like his father: dead at the hands of a Kozminski.

Out of respect for Mrs. Payne, Stacy motioned her brothers back, but they were already stepping away from Logan. They wouldn't touch him now—not in front of his mother. She couldn't promise they wouldn't exact some revenge later.

Even now she wondered…

Could one of them have fired those shots at the wedding? Her heart pounded heavily with dread and fear. She couldn't lose one of them like she'd lost her father—to prison. They had both already spent too much time behind bars.

And she couldn't lose Logan Payne, either. Not for herself. She didn't care about him. But his mother loved him. And it would kill her to lose a child like she'd lost her husband.

Mrs. Payne swung her hand toward that child's face. His reflexes weren't fast enough to stop her palm from connecting with his cheek. It wasn't quite a slap but a very forceful pat. "Why are *you* here?" she asked him.

"You must have heard the gunshots outside the church," he replied. "Somebody tried to kill me again."

Her hand trembled against his cheek, and she sucked in a shaky breath before asking, "Again?"

He groaned as if in regret at his slip or embarrassment of her concern. "Mom…"

Stacy's lips twitched at how close Logan Payne came to sounding like a petulant child. Even when he'd been a child of just seventeen at her father's trial, he had already seemed like a man. Strong. Intimidating. Independent.

"You don't need to be concerned," he assured his mother. "I'm putting a stop to it now. That's why I'm here."

"How is coming here putting a stop to anything?" Mrs. Payne asked, her usually smooth brow furrowed with confusion.

"You know how," he said.

"No, I don't." She shook her head.

"It's one of them," he insisted, but his gaze focused on Stacy.

"I don't understand," his mother continued. "Did you see one of them with the gun?"

Logan shook his head now.

"Then you have no business coming here today of all days," she said, "unless you've come to express your condolences and pay your respects."

"Is that why you're here?" he asked, his deep voice vibrating with betrayal. "Are you here to pay your respects to the man who killed your husband…who killed my father?"

Stacy's heart lurched with the pain in his voice. He was wrong about who'd taken his dad, but he'd still lost him, even sooner than she'd lost hers. At least she had been able to see her father the past fifteen years even though it had been behind bars.

"I am here for Stacy," Mrs. Payne replied, and her arm came around Stacy's shoulders.

She'd tried so hard to be strong—to be tough like her brothers and like Logan. But Mrs. Payne's warmth and affection crumbled the wall she'd built around herself so many years ago. Her shoulders began to shake like her knees had earlier.

"Is it okay with you that I'm here?" Mrs. Payne asked. "If it's too difficult, we'll all leave…"

"That would be best," a woman chimed in.

Stacy glanced up to see her aunt and uncle walking down the aisle toward them. Aunt Marta was tall and thin with frosted blond hair and a frosty personality. Uncle Iwan's hair had thinned while his body had widened. He was a big, imposing man, but he smiled at her. Aunt Marta glared. That look wasn't meant for Mrs. Payne but for Stacy. She'd been on the receiving end of it many times, but she was not yet immune to the coldness and shivered.

Mrs. Payne wrapped her arm more tightly around her, as if protecting her. She had done that in court fifteen years ago. A new widow then, she had still found sympathy for the daughter of the man convicted of killing her husband. Mrs. Payne had attended other court dates in Stacy's life—offering her support when Milek and Garek had faced their charges.

Stacy clutched at the older woman's waist. "Please," she murmured through the emotion choking her, "please stay…"

Mrs. Payne nodded. "Whatever you need, honey…"

Logan reached out a hand for his mother as if to tug her away from Stacy. He did not have Mrs. Payne's forgiving soul and warm heart. He was full of hatred and bitterness. But then his fingers curled into his palm and he pulled back his hand.

"We'll discuss this later," he said.

Stacy knew he spoke to her, not his mother, and

his words were a threat. He still considered her and her family responsible for the attempts on his life. And she wasn't entirely convinced he was wrong, especially with the way her brothers eyed him. He wasn't the only one in that church who was full of hatred and bitterness.

For the next hour those feelings were put aside, though, for grief and loss during the funeral mass and burial. While the others left for the funeral luncheon at what had been her father's favorite pub, she stayed behind at his grave site.

But she was not alone. She stared down at the fresh dirt covering her father's grave. A light breeze fluttered the leaves in the trees and tumbled the loose soil across the grave. She shivered at the cold, but it wasn't the breeze chilling her. It was the loss.

"I'm sorry," Mrs. Payne said. She hadn't gone with the others to the pub. She had stayed behind with Stacy, continuing to offer her support and sympathy. If only Stacy's own mother was as loving and affectionate…

But she was like Aunt Marta—she loved money and herself more than anyone else. Even her own children…

Stacy shook her head. "You have no reason to apologize."

"I am apologizing for my son," Mrs. Payne explained.

Knowing how much Logan would hate that,

Stacy smiled and finally pulled her gaze away from the ground to face the older woman. "He's thirty-two years old. His mother should not be making apologies for him any longer."

Mrs. Payne smiled, too. "*She* has to when he's too stubborn to do it himself."

"He doesn't think he has a reason to apologize," Stacy pointed out. "He thinks he's right." He always thought he was right.

"You are not responsible for those attempts on his life," Mrs. Payne defended her.

The woman's faith in Stacy warmed her heart. Not many other people in her life had trusted her so fully.

"No, I'm not," she said. Just like her father, she was not a killer.

Mrs. Payne's eyes were warm and brown but they had the same intensity of her son's blue eyes as her gaze focused on Stacy's face. "But you're not entirely certain someone in your family didn't fire those shots."

Stacy sucked in a breath of shock. Had Mrs. Payne really been offering her support, or had she been manipulating her into betraying her brothers?

"I can see your doubts."

Like her, they blamed Logan for their father's death. He hadn't put the shiv in him, but he had made certain that he stayed in prison long enough that someone else had. Her brothers had even suggested that Logan might have hired the other inmate to commit the murder. She didn't believe that; she knew Logan hadn't wanted her father dead. He'd just wanted him to suffer. And he hadn't cared that she'd suffered, too. Her brothers had cared, though—maybe too much.

But in reply to Mrs. Payne's remark, Stacy shook her head again in denial. She would not betray her brothers. She owed them too much: her life.

"I don't expect you to admit it," Mrs. Payne said. "You're too loyal for that—too protective of them."

She wasn't nearly as protective of them as her brothers were of her. They had sacrificed so much to keep her safe. She would do the same.

"And you're protective of your son," Stacy said. She'd seen how shaken the woman had been that there had been attempts on his life. "Is that why you're here?"

"I'm here for you," Mrs. Payne insisted. "But if Logan is right..." She shuddered. "I can't lose him like I lost his father." She reached out again and took Stacy's hand in hers. "And I don't want you to lose your brothers, either."

Tears of frustration stung Stacy's eyes. "I can't..."

But as Mrs. Payne had seen, she already doubted them. Even if they weren't the ones attempting to kill him, they could be picked up on suspicion because they'd been so angry and so vocal about their hatred of Logan. She swallowed a lump of emotion. "I'll talk to them, make sure that they're not behind the shootings."

Mrs. Payne sighed. "It's too bad you have to have that conversation—that you have to show them you doubt them, that you think they could be responsible, that you think they could be killers."

After all they'd done for her, she didn't want to hurt them any more than they were already hurting. They had lost their father, too. "Then what do I do?"

Mrs. Payne squeezed her hand. "You marry him."

"What?" She couldn't have heard her right. It was like the words her father had uttered on his dying breath—incomprehensible.

"Your brothers would never do anything to hurt you," Mrs. Payne said. "So if they believe you're in love with Logan, they won't hurt him."

"I—I can't convince them of such a blatant lie…"

"You can if you marry him…"

Marry the man she despised more than any other? It just wasn't conceivable. She wasn't the only one shocked and appalled at such a terrible union.

A deep gasp drew her attention away from Mrs. Payne to her son. Logan stood near a monument behind her. His blue eyes were wide with shock and horror at his mother's outrageous suggestion. Then his lips began to move. But no words were uttered, or if they were, the shots drowned out his voice.

Gunshots reverberated throughout the cemetery, echoing around the monuments and trees. The sudden loud noise sent the birds flying from the tree limbs to form a dark cloud in the sky above them.

Not only had Logan Payne intruded on her father's funeral but so had his killer. Mrs. Payne's plan was never going to happen, because Stacy would probably wind up burying him before she could ever marry him.

Chapter Three

Pain gripped Logan's shoulder, but he ignored the hot streak down his arm as he reached for his holster and drew his weapon. "Get down!" he shouted.

His mother had instinctively ducked behind a cement monument. But Stacy stood still at her father's freshly dug grave, so when he knocked her down, she hit soft ground. Her breath left her lips in a gasp of warm air that caressed his neck.

And her soft curves cushioned his fall. She always acted so strong that he had expected her to be hard and cold. But she was soft and warm. She was also smaller than her big personality and more fragile than her tough attitude.

"Are you okay?" he asked as the shots continued to ring out, knocking leaves and twigs from the trees so they rained down on them like debris during a hurricane. For some reason he felt as though he were in the middle of a storm and not just of gunfire but of emotion.

Had his mother really suggested what he'd

thought he heard? No. He must have misconstrued her words. Not even she was a big enough matchmaker to consider a marriage between him and Stacy Kozminski at all possible.

Stacy stared up at him through gray eyes wide with shock but hopefully not pain.

"Were you hit?" he asked. "Are you hurt?"

Eyes still wide, she finally moved as she shook her head.

"Mom?" he called out. "Mom?"

"I—I'm okay," she replied, but her voice cracked with fear. As usual, it wasn't for herself as she anxiously asked, "Are you and Stacy okay?"

"Yeah…" He shifted, moving to roll off Stacy and return fire now that he knew she and his mother were safe. But Stacy gripped his shoulder, and he flinched in pain.

"You've been shot," she said, her voice breaking with urgency and concern. For him?

He shrugged his shoulders, but there was a twinge of pain. Maybe more than a twinge. He grimaced and lied, "I'm fine."

"You're bleeding," she said. Her palm smeared with his blood, she lifted it toward his face as if presenting him with evidence.

He didn't need to see it; he could feel it, sticking his sleeve to his skin. He glanced down then and noted the tear in the shoulder of his tuxedo jacket.

Oh, Mom was going to be annoyed that he'd ruined another one...

"Are—are you hurt?" his mother asked, and unconcerned about her own safety, she began to rise from behind the monument.

"Stay down," he warned her.

"The shooting stopped," she pointed out.

But that didn't mean that the shooter was gone. He could have just been biding his time until he got a clear shot. And if someone really wanted to hurt Logan, he or she could do that most effectively by hurting his mother.

"Stay down," he told her again. "Don't move until we get backup." Maybe he shouldn't have convinced Parker and Nikki and Candace that he didn't need their protection. Maybe he should have let them stay with him like they'd wanted. Knowing them, they might have ignored his wishes—like his mother usually did.

Sirens wailed as police cars approached, lights flashing through the tree branches.

Stacy stiffened beneath him. Apparently, she had inherited her family's aversion to law enforcement. "Your backup has arrived."

To him, backup was his family and employees. But the police would do. He doubted they would apprehend the shooter, though. His mother was right; he was gone. He'd gotten away again.

He rolled off Stacy and stood up. Then he extended his uninjured arm to her. She stared at his hand before putting hers into it. Her hand was small and delicate inside his but not so delicate that she didn't have calluses.

"Maybe there will be an ambulance, too," she said.

"I don't need one."

"You were shot."

"You were shot?" his mother asked, her voice shrill with alarm as she rushed over to him.

"I was just grazed," he assured them. "There's no bullet in me." This time. But every attempt got a little closer, a little more successful. The shooter wasn't going to stop until Logan was dead.

STACY WAS FURIOUS and for once her anger wasn't directed at Logan Payne. Her heels clicking against the slate floor, she stomped across the crowded pub to the knotty pine-paneled back room where her family was drinking a farewell toast to her father.

Or was their farewell to Logan? Was one of them the shooter? Did he realize that he'd hit him? Maybe he thought he'd killed him.

He could have killed Mrs. Payne, too. Hell, with as wildly as he'd been firing, he could have killed *her*. If Logan had ducked faster, the bullet that had hit him might have struck her instead. His reflexes had slowed at the wrong time for him, but the right time for her.

She shuddered but refused to give in to the fear that had paralyzed her at the cemetery. Anger was better; it made her stronger.

"Stacy!" Milek greeted her with a hug, his eyes bright with the sheen of inebriation. He was the lightweight of the family and could only handle a drink or two.

She slammed her palms into his chest, shoving him back with such force that he nearly fell over. But Garek, also standing at the bar, grabbed him and kept him upright.

"What the hell!" he protested.

"What the hell!" she yelled back at him. She didn't care if she hurt their feelings now. She was so pissed over getting shot at that she actually understood Logan Payne intruding on her father's funeral. "Which one of you idiots shot up the cemetery?"

"What?" Garek asked.

"I nearly got shot," she said.

"What! Are you okay?" Milek asked, grabbing for her again.

She jerked back. "I'm fine."

"It must have been Logan Payne," Milek murmured. "He must have shot at you..." A look passed between him and his brother—a look of rage and revenge.

"No," she said, in response to that look as much as her brother's statement. "Logan Payne is the one who got shot!" As if they didn't already know that…

"What's going on?" Aunt Marta asked. "This is inappropriate talk for a funeral…" She sniffed her disdain of her husband's niece and nephews. She had never approved of them because they were a convict's children. Her own husband was a criminal but since he had never been caught, he wasn't as unseemly as his brother and his offspring—mostly because of the lavish lifestyle his actions afforded her.

"Is Payne dead?" Milek asked.

Stacy's stomach pitched as she remembered the blood on his tuxedo. She shook her head. "No."

His mother had forced him to go to the hospital to make certain that the bullet had only grazed him as he'd claimed. Mrs. Payne had wanted Stacy to ride along—probably so that she could propose marriage between Stacy and her son again. Even if she talked Stacy into her outrageous plan, there was no way in hell that Logan would ever agree to become her husband—even if it were only pretend.

"That's too bad," Milek murmured with regret that Logan lived.

Had Milek been the shooter? Was that why he was drinking so heavily? Or was drinking his way of mourning their father?

Stacy wanted to mourn their father, too, but she'd hardly had the chance between Logan and the shooting. Before she could say anything else to her brothers, Aunt Marta grasped her arm and tugged her aside. Probably for another lecture on funereal etiquette.

"Why are you so angry with your brothers?" she asked.

Why was she so angry? Was it because if they were the shooters, they were risking prison again? Or was it because if they were the shooters, they were trying to kill Logan Payne?

She shook her head. "I'm not…"

"They are struggling with your father's loss," Aunt Marta said. "They didn't get the chance to say goodbye that you got."

"They could have stayed behind at the cemetery." She suspected at least one of them probably had…

"At the prison," Aunt Marta said. "The warden called you to see your father…"

She almost wished she had been spared seeing him like that, but he had asked for her. He had wanted to talk to her. She shuddered now as she remembered seeing him as she had, in so much pain, his life slipping away from him…

"What did he say to you?" her aunt asked.

Stacy tilted her head in confusion, uncertain that she'd heard the older woman correctly. They had never been close—at her aunt's choosing. She was hardly going to share any secrets with the woman now. "Why do you care?"

"I'm just curious…"

The woman was too self-absorbed to be curious about anyone but herself. She only wanted to know about things that might affect her. Why did she think Stacy's father's last words might concern her?

Stacy had no intention of satisfying the woman's morbid curiosity, so she turned away from her. But Aunt Marta grasped her arm in her talonlike fingers and asked again, "What did he say to you?"

The woman was persistent, or as Uncle Iwan would admit when he had too much to drink, a nag. She wasn't going to give up until Stacy gave her an answer. Any answer might do…

So she shook her head. "I couldn't understand him…"

Aunt Marta expelled a little breath—as if she were relieved. Had her brother-in-law taken one of her secrets to his grave?

Stacy had actually misled her aunt. She'd understood what her father had said, she just hadn't understood *why* he'd said it. When he'd spoken them, Stacy had put no credence in her father's last words. She'd blamed the strange statement on the painkillers they'd given him to make him comfortable because they hadn't been able to do anything else to treat his injury.

She still didn't understand why he'd said what he had…

"Son of a—!" Garek said as he turned toward the entrance to the pub's back room.

Logan Payne walked in as if he'd been invited. But Garek had been right to stop himself from finishing his curse. Mrs. Payne was the sweetest woman Stacy had ever met—the most forgiving and generous woman—and probably one of the smartest, as well.

"I thought you got shot," Milek drunkenly murmured. Had he thought that because of what Stacy had said or because he'd thought he'd hit him?

Logan probably wondered the same thing, because his eyes narrowed with suspicion. He gestured toward the tear in the shoulder of the tuxedo he still wore. It was even more rumpled and smudged with dirt and blood now. "The bullet barely grazed me," he replied. Then, with a sneer that was somehow both infuriating and sexy as hell, he added, "Somebody's a lousy shot."

Garek chuckled. "Then it can't be any one of us who's shooting at you. We would have hit you by now."

Despite her brother's bravado, neither he nor Milek were expert marksmen. They weren't killers, either, even though they had actually killed before. And if Logan kept goading them, they might kill again—right here.

Stacy had to do something to diffuse the potentially dangerous situation. It wouldn't be just dangerous for Logan, who was outnumbered, it would be dangerous for her brothers, too, because if they hurt him—or worse—they would go back to prison.

"Why the hell do you keep showing up where you're not wanted?" Aunt Marta demanded to know. This time her disdain was for the intruder. She usually considered her brother-in-law's children intruders, too, even though they were blood.

"He's wanted," Stacy said suddenly. She'd realized what she had to do back at the cemetery, maybe even before the gunshots had rang out. But in this moment, she made the quick decision that she was actually going to go through with it. "I want him here..."

Curving her lips into a big smile, she crossed the room to where he stood. His long body was tense. His face tight, he looked stunned, as if he'd been shot again—and that was just from what she'd said. She had no idea how he would react to what she was about to do. Maybe he would stop her before she could even act, like he had when she'd tried to slap him. But he just stood there when she wrapped her arms around his neck.

Why hadn't he stopped her? Why hadn't he caught her arms and pushed her away? He stared down at her, his blue eyes intense and watchful as he waited for her next move.

Could she...?

Bracing herself for what she had to do, she drew in a deep breath. Then she rose up on tiptoe and pressed a kiss to his hard-looking lips. But they weren't hard. They were surprisingly pliant and sensual and fuller than they looked in the tight line of disapproval into which they were usually drawn.

Now she was the one who was stunned—because he kissed her back. He clamped one arm, probably his uninjured one, around her back and pulled her tightly against him. Then he parted her lips and deepened the kiss.

Noise erupted in the room. Gasps. Shouts. Even a scream. But she could barely hear them for the blood rushing through her head, roaring in her ears. Her pulse pounded madly with adrenaline and attraction. Had it been so long since she'd been kissed that any man could affect her like this? It couldn't be just because it was Logan. She couldn't want a man that she hated as much as this one.

But no man had ever kissed her like he was kissing her—with so much passion and desire that her knees weakened and her head swam and she completely forgot why she'd kissed him in the first place.

When he pulled back, she was panting for breath.

Against her lips, he murmured, "What the hell are you up to?"

For a moment she couldn't remember. Then it came back to her—the plan, his mother's outrageous plan.

She whispered back, "I'm saving your life." She turned toward her stunned family and announced, "Logan Payne is my fiancé. We're getting married."

Chapter Four

Logan's heart pounded so hard that it was the only sound in the sudden silence that had fallen after Stacy's insane announcement. He knew his mother had initially proposed this crazy engagement, but he hadn't expected that Stacy would ever agree to it. She hated him.

But he hadn't tasted that hatred on her lips when she'd kissed him so convincingly that even he had forgotten it wasn't real. He knew that she didn't really want him; she just didn't want her brothers going to prison for killing him. She was protecting Milek and Garek—not Logan.

So then she couldn't be behind the attempts on his life. Or maybe she had been, but his mother's idea had convinced Stacy to change her plan for revenge to one for marriage. But then marrying him might be more vengeful than killing him.

Not that he was going to fall in with his mother's crazy plan. He wasn't about to get coerced into marriage with a woman he couldn't…

Stand? More like resist. Why had he kissed her back? To punish her for the game she was playing? He'd like to think that but he had enjoyed it too damn much. Her mouth was so sweet and so damn sexy when it moved over his.

"What the hell is going on?" one of her brothers, his face flushed either with alcohol or temper, demanded to know. "Just a couple of hours ago you were mad at him for crashing Dad's funeral and now you're engaged?"

Her other brother's eyes narrowed, he glared at Logan. "He must be threatening her."

"He saved my life at the cemetery," she said. "He took a bullet for me."

He was pretty sure that bullet had been meant for him and that one of her brothers had fired it. And that was the only reason he was refraining from calling her on her lie. As her fake fiancé, he had access to her family—hopefully enough access to gather evidence. Like the damn gun they kept firing at him…

She continued, "It was all very sudden."

"It's all B.S.," he whispered back at her.

She grabbed his hand and squeezed it. Hard. And he was surprised again that she had calluses on her small hands. What did she do for a living or for fun that had produced such calluses?

They were *engaged* and yet he hardly knew Stacy Kozminski.

"I'm surprised myself at the feelings I have for—" her throat moved, as if she were choking on his name or maybe just on her lie "—Logan."

Despite that kiss, he doubted her feelings had changed. She still hated him.

One of her brothers—Garek—voiced his sentiment. "You hate his guts, Stace."

She shook her head. "That's not true."

"You've said over and over that you hate his guts," Garek persisted. "Why are you lying about it now? What's he got on you?"

What did he think Logan could have on her? Proof that she and her brothers were responsible for the shootings? He hoped like hell he had it, then he could call her on her lie and end this nonsense. Then he could call the police...

"My gratitude," she said. "He saved my life." She turned toward him and glanced up. Maybe her gaze was supposed to be adoring, but she just looked miserable. "He's my hero."

Garek snorted. "And that just erases everything else he's done to our father?"

Her snotty aunt added, "To our family? You're betraying your father. Your uncle. Your brothers..."

Ignoring her aunt, she replied to her brother only, "I understand why he's done what he has."

"I don't understand what you think you're doing," Logan murmured. Her family was never going to buy that she'd had such a drastic change of heart over *him*.

"If the situation was reversed," she continued as if he hadn't spoken, "we would have done the same. Or more…"

"He killed our father," Milek said, his words slurred. He had definitely been drinking. "And you're rewarding him for it."

"Logan did not kill Dad," Stacy defended him. "Some gang member did."

"He wouldn't have had the chance if your boy-friend—"

"Fiancé," she corrected her brother. "And stop. Just stop…all of it." She turned toward Logan. "It's been a long day. Please, take me home."

Did she mean his home? He wasn't about to bring her there. She would probably set it on fire. And he had no idea where she lived. But instead of asking any questions in front of her resentful family, he escorted her out of the pub.

"Have you been drinking with your brother?" he asked as he opened the passenger door for her.

"I'm not drunk," she said. Her gray eyes were clear as she glared at him.

"Then why on earth—"

"We can't talk about it here," she said. "There are cameras in the lot."

Her paranoia lifted his brows with surprise. "And you think your brothers would look at the footage?"

"I don't know about them," she said. "But I wouldn't put it past my aunt." She stepped on the running board of his SUV, but her heel slipped and she fell back against him. His arms closed around her, and he lifted her easily onto the seat. Maybe she was as exhausted as she'd claimed because she didn't fight him. Or maybe she was just worried about what her aunt might see on the security cameras.

"Okay, I'll drive you home," he said.

She waited until he rounded the front bumper and slid behind the wheel before she replied, "It's the least you can do since I'm saving your life."

"So you admit my life is in danger because of you?" His suspicions had obviously not been unfounded. He pushed aside the guilt he'd been feeling for interrupting her father's funeral to confront her. And it wasn't just his mother who'd made him feel guilty but Stacy had, too—with all the pain he'd seen in her gray eyes.

She was mourning. He understood that; he'd spent the past fifteen years mourning the loss of his father. Hers was to blame for that, but *she* wasn't. Maybe for the first time in fifteen years he realized that.

She emitted a soft, shaky sigh. "I'm not admitting anything, Detective Payne."

"I haven't been a detective for a few years." Not since he'd started Payne Protection Agency.

"I think you'll always be a detective," she replied.

"If I was, I wouldn't have to ask where you live," he pointed out. "I would already know."

She arched her brows in surprise. She must have assumed he knew. But Logan was just realizing how very little he actually knew about his fake fiancée. He had been so focused on what her father had done that he'd never paid attention to what she had done. Or what she was doing…

What was she doing? And not just with her life but with him? Why was she willing to pretend she was in love with him? What was her real agenda?

"I'll tell you where I live," she said. "But we have to stop somewhere else first."

Maybe her agreeing to his mother's plan was just a ruse for her to get him alone—somewhere that she would have no witnesses to her killing him.

WONDERING WHICH ONE would attack first, Stacy studied the two alpha males with which she shared the relatively small confines of the SUV. Cujo sat on the backseat, but the German shepherd's black-and-tan body was so long that his head reached over the console. She scratched him behind his droopy ear, and he whined and licked her face.

"I missed you, too," she murmured.

"Why'd you have him at the kennel?" Logan asked. He had obviously been surprised that was the place she'd had him stop before taking her home.

"Because I've been staying with a friend since my dad died," she said.

"And that friend didn't want *Cujo* staying, too?" he asked with a derisive snort.

The German shepherd whipped his big head toward Logan and nudged his shoulder with his nose. The SUV swerved a little before Logan gripped the wheel more tightly. "What he'd do that for?"

She chuckled. "That's his name."

"Cujo?"

The dog barked and then nudged him again. Logan held his hand between them, letting the canine sniff him before petting his head. If Cujo had been a cat, he might have purred.

"Traitor," she teased him. The dog had apparently conceded which one of them was the true alpha male. She wasn't surprised it was Logan. Since he was the boss of the family business, his brothers and sister must have conceded he was the alpha male, too.

"That's probably what your family is saying about you now," Logan said. "That you're the traitor."

Her stomach churned with nerves. They were the only thing in it. She hadn't been able to eat since she'd seen her father in the prison infirmary. "Probably."

"So why did you claim to be my fiancée?" he

asked. "Because you know your brothers have been trying to kill me?"

She shook her head. "I don't know any such thing."

"Liar," he softly accused her.

She should have been offended but *liar* was the least of his insults. He thought she was a killer, too. "You really think I put out a hit on you and hired my brothers to do it?"

"You wouldn't need to hire them," he replied. "They'll do whatever you tell them to."

That was what she was counting on—to keep them from killing Logan Payne. "If I wanted you dead, why would I tell them that I'm going to marry you?"

"You want to be able to collect my life insurance," he suggested, "as my widow."

"Hmm," she mock-mused, "I hadn't considered that." She nodded as if committing to the idea like she was going to try to make everyone believe she was going to commit to him. "At least then I'll get something out of this marriage."

He glanced at her, his blue gaze hot and intense. "If we were actually going to get married, you'd definitely get something out of it."

Her heart flipped. "Are you flirting with me, Logan Payne?"

"Isn't that what a *fiancé* is supposed to do?"

She shrugged. "I have no idea. I've never been

engaged." She didn't even date that often. That had to be why kissing him had affected her so much.

"Me, neither," he said.

"Why not?" she asked.

His mouth curved into a grin. "Do you think I'm way too handsome to still be single?"

Yes. But she would eat Cujo's kibble before she would ever admit that she found Logan Payne attractive. But she always had. Even during her father's trial, her brothers had accused her of having a crush on him because she hadn't been able to stop herself from staring at him.

But she replied with an insult, "I think you're pretty old to still be single."

He laughed. "You're only a few years younger than I am. Starting to feel like an old maid at twenty-nine? Is that why you jumped at my mother's crazy idea to marry me?"

"Your mother." Unable to help herself, she smiled with genuine affection for Mrs. Payne. "She's another reason I'm surprised you're still single. She's a *wedding* planner."

"And a matchmaker." He sighed. "She's the reason my brother just got married."

"She manipulated him into it?"

He nodded.

"I feel badly for the bride, then." She could commiserate with that whole manipulation thing.

"Why?" he asked. "You don't even know my

brother Cooper. He enlisted in the marines out of high school and just came home a few days ago."

"Cooper? He's the one who was named after your father's partner?" She shivered at just the thought of implacable Officer Robert Cooper and how his testimony had helped seal her father's fate.

A muscle twitched along Logan's jaw and he nodded.

She shouldn't have brought up his father again. Even fifteen years later, he still felt the loss. So she had no hope of her grief ever lessening. But she would deal with that later—when she wasn't worried about losing her brothers, too.

"I don't know your brother," she agreed. "But I feel sorry for his bride because he doesn't love her."

"Oh, he loves her." Logan chuckled. "He's been in love with her since they were in high school together."

"So your mother really didn't manipulate him into marrying her, then." Maybe the woman wasn't some matchmaking mastermind.

"Oh, she did," he said. "Cooper's so stubborn he probably would have never admitted to his feelings."

"Stubborn or cowardly?" she asked.

Logan chuckled. "He's a highly decorated marine."

She shrugged. "Even a brave man can be a coward when it comes to love…"

"Sounds like you have a story about that," he mused. "Is it about your *friend?*" He'd said "friend" as if it meant something more than friendship and almost as if he was jealous that it might be.

"Why would you ask that?" And why would he sound jealous when he asked?

"I didn't see any friends at the funeral," he explained almost nonchalantly, "just your family."

"That's why my friend couldn't come," she said, "because of my family."

"He has a problem with your brothers, too?"

She nodded but didn't bother correcting his misconception about the gender of her *friend.* Maybe she had only imagined his jealousy, but if he actually was, she liked it—which was odd since she didn't like him. Sure, she found him attractive—maybe she was even attracted to him—but she still didn't like him.

"Even if I agreed to it, my mother's plan would never work," Logan warned her.

She was afraid of that, too, because she would have to convince her family that she loved a man she really couldn't stand. And she was no actress—she'd never even been very good at lying.

"And really, all you have to do to stop them from trying to kill me is to tell them to stop," he said, "because they'll do what you tell them to."

If only that were true…then she wouldn't have to fake an engagement, or heaven forbid, a marriage, if it actually came to that. And it might take marriage to convince her family that she was committed to Logan Payne.

"I'm not so sure about that," she reluctantly admitted.

"Then even you realize they're dangerously out of control," Logan said.

"I never said that!" she exclaimed, horrified that she might have inadvertently implicated her brothers. And, like Logan, she had no proof they were behind the attempts on his life. But thanks to Logan and the threats they'd previously made, she now had doubts.

"They've already tried to kill me. More than once," he insisted. "They need to be brought to justice."

"You have no evidence," she reminded him.

"I'll find it," he warned her.

"I buried my father today," she said, her voice cracking with the emotion that overwhelmed her. "Isn't that enough justice for you?"

Cujo whined and nudged her with his head, as if trying to comfort her. Surprisingly, he wasn't the only one because Logan's hand covered hers on the dog's fur.

"I'm sorry you're hurting," he said.

But he wasn't sorry that her father was dead and he was determined to arrest her brothers. He wasn't sorry about any of that…

She pulled her hand out from beneath his. If she couldn't stand his touch, how was she going to convince her family that she loved him? But then she'd had no problem with his touch earlier when he'd kissed her. Her lips still tingled from the electricity of that contact with his.

"We're here," she said with a sigh of relief as she just realized that he'd stopped the SUV outside her building. The street side of the ground floor held the storefront for her jewelry business, her workshop was in the back, and her apartment was above it. It wasn't the greatest neighborhood; that was why she needed Cujo. Even now a car alarm blared and police sirens whined in the distance.

Logan peered through the window and murmured, "This is really where you live?"

She'd never taken Logan Payne for a snob. "You mean because I'm the daughter of a jewelry thief and I live above a jewelry store?"

"I'm surprised you admit he was a thief," he said.

"He was a thief," she said. He'd always been honest about that. "But he wasn't a killer…"

Logan rubbed his temple and groaned as if sick of hearing it. But maybe if he heard it enough he would come to believe it. "I was actually referring to the dangerous neighborhood," he said as he continued to look around like a cop assessing the potential dangers of his beat. "Now I understand why you have the dog."

"Your mother is actually the one who brought me Cujo," she said. After the older woman had heard about her store being robbed, she'd talked an old friend of her deceased husband into giving the German shepherd to Stacy. "He was a K-9 cop."

"He doesn't look old enough to have been retired," Logan said as he scratched behind the dog's ear, which Cujo loved.

"He was shot," she said. "In the shoulder..." Like Logan had been shot. No wonder the two alpha males had come so quickly to an understanding. They were actually quite alike. Cujo wasn't always that nice or polite, either. That was why her friend hadn't wanted the dog staying with her, too—especially since he might have thought her Pomeranian was a squirrel. Cujo really hated squirrels.

Logan leaned his head against the dog and imitated the way Cujo nuzzled the few people he actually liked. "You're a hero," he praised the canine cop.

"He saved his partner," she said.

"That's what a partner is supposed to do," Logan murmured.

Somehow she suspected he wasn't talking about the partnership of their proposed marriage. "You're not going to do it, are you?"

"Marry you?" He shook his head. "It's a bad idea. And as I already pointed out, it would never work."

He was probably right. But she couldn't agree

with him without a fight. She'd been fighting with Logan Payne too long to concede defeat. "That's your fault," she accused him.

His mouth curved into a sexy grin. "Are you saying that kiss wasn't convincing?"

If she said it wasn't, he might kiss her again— might try to prove how convincing he could be. She was tempted to lie because she was tempted…to kiss him again. But instead she shook her head and clarified, "It's your fault for being such a jerk all these years that they would never believe I could actually fall for you."

"And so they'll keep trying to kill me."

"Is that why you didn't give me up as a liar back at the pub?" she asked. "You were afraid you weren't going to get out of there alive?"

"I'm not afraid of your brothers," he said with a snort of disgust.

She was afraid of what they might do, of what they might have already done. They would do anything for her, and even though she hadn't asked them, she'd given them every reason to think she wanted Logan Payne dead. She needed to give them a reason to leave him alive—like their fake engagement.

She glanced around as Logan had, but she was looking for her brothers. They might have followed them from the pub. "You need to walk me to my door," she said.

"I thought you had the dog to keep you safe," he said. "Not that you're the one in danger..."

"I don't want you to keep me safe," she said. She wanted to keep him safe. Actually, she wanted to keep her brothers safe from themselves. "I want my fiancé to walk me to my door."

He uttered an exasperated-sounding sigh. "Stacy, I'm not playing along with my mother's plan."

"Do you want me to tell her—?"

"You can tell her—"

"—that her son is not enough of a gentleman to walk a lady to her door," she continued as if he hadn't interrupted her.

He groaned. But he opened his door and walked around to open hers.

Cujo jumped down with her and led the way to the back stairwell. She fumbled in her purse before unlocking the door. Cujo's ears perked up, and a low growl emanated from his throat.

"He smells something," Logan said, and he was already pulling his gun from beneath his jacket, wincing only slightly at the strain on his wound. "Someone may have broken into your place."

"And locked the door behind himself?" she scoffed. "I doubt that."

The dog hurried ahead—with Logan in hot pursuit. "Stay outside," he ordered her.

But she didn't take orders from Logan Payne. He wasn't her boss. He had even refused to be her fake fiancé. So she followed. And then saw what Cujo had found: a pipe bomb sat on her kitchen table, red numbers blinking as the timer quickly counted down.

Chapter Five

The bomb went off with such force that it blew the lid off the bomb unit's transfer container. The stairwell rattled, boards giving away beneath the weight of the ATF agents and that container. The agents tumbled down to the concrete alley.

Logan's hand shook in reaction. He'd touched that damn thing. He'd defused it or at least he'd stopped the clock—a clock that hadn't begun its countdown until they'd stepped inside the apartment and activated it. After stopping the timer, he'd called ATF to dispose of the device since explosives often went off when moved. At least it hadn't blown up him and Stacy and her dog. The two of them crouched behind his SUV with him. Her arms wrapped tightly around the dog, Stacy held Cujo either to protect the canine or to thank him for protecting her.

He reached out and petted the dog's head. "You're a hero again, buddy."

"Are they all right?" Stacy asked after the welfare of the ATF agents.

He glanced back to where the agents scrambled to their feet. "Looks like nobody got hurt." Thank goodness for their protective gear and that container that had absorbed most of the explosion.

"What about my place?"

He hesitated until she grasped his arm. A twinge of pain shot through his wounded shoulder. He then realized maybe the bullet hadn't been intended for him at all. Maybe he hadn't been the intended target at the cemetery—just like he hadn't been the intended target of the bomb, either.

She jerked her hand away and said, "I'm sorry. I forgot you were hurt."

So had he.

She shuddered. "You could have been hurt so much worse," she said. "I can't believe you touched the bomb…"

He suppressed a shudder of his own revulsion. "Me, neither."

"It's a miracle you didn't get killed."

Especially given how easily the bomb had gone off in transport. "When my brother Cooper first got back home, I picked his brain for everything he'd learned in the service." Of course Cooper had thought that Logan was stalling giving him a real assignment or interviewing him to see if he was ready to take one. Cooper had already proven he was ready. And he'd even saved Logan's life after he'd left for his honeymoon. "He showed me and Parker how to defuse an improvised explosive device."

"He thought that was something you'd need to know?" she asked, her brow furrowing in confusion.

Actually Logan had thought that. "Payne Protection Agency promises to protect our clients from all dangers—even bombs."

"You protected me," she said, "and I'm not even your client."

"Maybe you should be," he said, "because someone just tried to blow you up. Who would do that and why?"

Her lips parted, and a ragged breath slipped out, but no words. And before she could form any, they were interrupted.

"Stacy!" a deep voice shouted as her brother Garek pushed through the police barricade set up around the perimeter of her building. An officer attempted to stop him, but he—with the help of Milek—pushed past him.

Logan held up a hand to the officer, verifying that it was okay to let them through. Okay for Stacy, anyway. He doubted that her brothers would ever hurt her. They loved her so much that they were distraught, their eyes wild with worry over finding the police barricade around her place. Maybe they'd heard the explosion, too.

"Are you all right?" Garek asked as he dragged her into his arms.

She clung to him, trembling. "Yes. Yes."

"This is your fault!" Milek told Logan. "This is your danger you've dragged her into with you!"

Logan shook his head, but before he could defend himself, Stacy pulled free of Garek and whirled toward Milek, who must have sobered up, because his eyes were clear now and his face pale. She poked his chest with a finger.

"You should be thanking him for saving my life again!" she shouted at her brother. "If Logan hadn't stopped that bomb from going off, it would have killed us!"

"Stopped the bomb?" Garek scoffed. "Your damn stairwell has been blown off the building! You could have been killed."

"The ATF agents set it off when they were moving it," Logan explained.

"My stairwell is gone?" Stacy glanced back at the building and shuddered. "That could have been us…"

"It was supposed to be you," Logan said. "The bomb was set inside your apartment." And it was impossible that the bomb was intended to harm Logan because no one—not even her brothers—could have guessed that he would have driven her home. Stacy hadn't announced their fake engagement until that afternoon. And even if they'd known he might step foot inside her apartment, he doubted that they would have risked her life even to take his.

So he wasn't the only one someone was trying to kill. Apparently, someone wanted Stacy Kozminski dead, as well.

STACY SHIVERED. SHE wasn't cold even though goose bumps lifted on her arms and the back of her neck beneath the heavy fall of her hair. Her skin was tingling because of Logan Payne's stare. He stood several feet away, deep in conversation with the ATF agents, but his gaze was on her, as if he was reluctant to let her out of his sight.

She had already spoken with them, answering all their questions the best that she could. Given that she hadn't been home since her dad died at the prison, she'd had no idea when or how someone had broken into her apartment to set the bomb. And she had absolutely no idea why.

Logan conversed with the agents now. He was probably the one asking the questions instead of answering them. But as he talked, he watched her. While his stare unsettled her, it also—oddly enough—reassured her. He had already saved her life once. Maybe twice if those shots at the cemetery had actually been intended for her.

But why would someone try to shoot at her? Or worse yet, blow her up? Unable to comprehend why anyone would want her dead, she murmured, "Why?"

"That's a damn good question," Garek replied as if she'd asked it of him.

Maybe still in shock over nearly being killed, she just shook her head. "I have no idea."

"Then why would you agree to it?" Garek asked.

Even further confused, she turned toward her brother and asked, "Agree to what?"

"You and Logan Payne," he said. "Why are you claiming you're engaged to the guy?"

She glanced to Logan again. At least he was too far away to hear her lie again and contradict it. Yet. He would eventually deny their engagement, but until then she intended to perpetuate the lie. "It's the truth."

Garek shook his head. "You hate the guy's guts."

"That was once true," she admitted. Even that morning it had been true. But she didn't hate Logan anymore—not after he'd saved her. That would have been ungrateful or, at the very least, stupid. She owed him her life. And maybe she could repay him with his. "But my feelings for him have changed."

Milek snorted. "Yeah, right..."

"Even if your feelings for him have changed," Garek allowed, "his feelings for you couldn't have.

He's hated all of us for years because of what our father did to his."

"Our father didn't do anything to his," she insisted. Why was she the only one who believed in his innocence? How could his own sons doubt him?

Garek nodded sharply as if he was only humoring her. "Yeah, right, but Payne doesn't believe that."

That was definitely true. "But he doesn't hold us responsible," she insisted. Weakly. She really was a lousy liar.

"He always thinks the worst of us," Milek said. "He actually believes we've been shooting at him."

Despite Mrs. Payne's warning about hurting their feelings, Stacy had already accused them of shooting. But then they'd been drunk and she'd been angry. So now she kept her voice low and her gaze steady as she asked, "Have you?"

Garek sucked in a breath. "I guess your feelings for him really have changed," he said, "because you never would have listened to his suspicions before."

She might have listened, but she would have ignored them—even though she had never been able to ignore him. Even when she'd hated him…

Fully aware that her brother hadn't actually answered her question, she persisted, "Are they only suspicions?"

"Of course," Garek replied—as offended as she had been afraid he would be. His mouth pulled into a tight grimace of disgust, and he swallowed hard. "I can't believe you'd fall for Logan Payne..."

If she had, she would have been as disgusted with herself as her oldest brother was with her. But she couldn't let him see her true feelings, so she buried them deep and plastered on a dreamy smile.

"Why not?" she asked. "He's an amazing man."

"Amazing that he's still alive..." Milek murmured.

She shivered at her brother's ominous tone. Maybe he was just still drunk. He couldn't mean that he actually wanted Logan dead. But then maybe he did...

"Milek!" she admonished him. "That's a horrible thing to say."

He shrugged. "All I meant was that if someone has tried to kill him as many times as he claims, then it's amazing that they haven't succeeded."

Garek nodded. "It is amazing. But then we actually only have his word that these attempts were made on *his* life."

"I was there when he was shot at in the cemetery," she reminded them. And she had been so furious over it that she'd already accused them of being involved. They'd been drinking then and confused, so they probably hadn't realized that she'd already had her own suspicions.

"But was it really him they were shooting at?" Garek voiced her earlier fear. "Or was it you?"

She shrugged now. "I don't know about that, but I do know that Logan wasn't the one shooting at me. He saved me at the cemetery like he saved me just now when we discovered the bomb in my apartment."

Her legs began to shake as she remembered that mess of wires and pipes sitting in the middle of her kitchen table where usually she displayed a crystal bowl of fruit or a vase of flowers.

"Has it occurred to you that he was able to stop it from going off so easily because he'd concocted the damn thing?" Garek voiced his own suspicions.

"He was able to dismantle it because his brother—the former marine—had shown him how to disarm improvised explosive devices."

"If his brother Cooper knows how to take the bombs apart, he must know how to put them together," Garek said.

"And Parker could have been the one shooting at the cemetery," Milek added.

Maybe her brothers hadn't sobered up yet. "Why?" she asked. "Why would they try to kill their own brother and risking hurting their mother, too?" The Payne family had already suffered too much loss, and that loss had brought them closer together, had made them more protective of each other. Not murderous.

"I can think of quite a few reasons," Milek murmured with a resentful glare in Logan's direction.

"They weren't trying to kill him," Garek explained to her. "They were trying to kill *you*."

"Why?" she asked.

"Maybe they actually think your crazy engagement story is the truth and they're trying to stop the wedding," Garek said.

Even though it had been Mrs. Payne's idea, nobody in Logan's family knew about their fake engagement. And given Logan's opposition to it, they probably never would.

Garek continued, "But seriously, the Payne family would only act on the boss's orders."

"And Logan Payne is the boss," Milek added.

Maybe he was boss of Payne Protection, but Penny Payne was the boss of her family. And she would never allow any of her kids to hurt her. She knew how much Stacy had already been hurt. And so did her brothers.

They were only trying to protect her. And maybe they had reason to.

She really only had Logan's word that there had been other attempts on his life—attempts that hadn't involved her nearly getting shot or blown up, as well. She turned toward where he'd been standing with the ATF agents, but he was no longer there.

Then a strong arm curled around her shoulders

and pulled her tight to his side. She didn't mistake him for one of her brothers this time. She recognized his touch now. Her body recognized it as her pulse quickened. But that might not have been with attraction; that might have only been with fear. She couldn't, and shouldn't, trust him. Because, as her brothers had pointed out, his feelings for her couldn't have changed. He still hated her.

But then why did he hold her so closely, nearly molding her body against his? Just to mess with her? Did he realize how much his nearness affected her?

"Payne, what the hell do you think you're doing?" Garek asked as he glared at Logan with hatred darkening his gray eyes.

She couldn't trust her brothers, either—because Logan might be telling the truth about the attempts on his life and he might be right about who was behind them.

Instead of ignoring Garek's impudent question, Logan—equally as impudent—replied, "I'm taking my fiancée home."

She barely managed to contain her shock. He'd been adamant that his mother's plan would never work, so why was he playing along now? Or was he only playing—just amusing himself by aggravating her brothers?

Garek tensed and bristled like Cujo when he saw

a cat or a small dog or a squirrel. His upper lip curled, he barked back, "She is home."

With the stairwell blown off the side of the building, it didn't look much like home. But she could still access her second-story apartment through the inside stairwell.

"The ATF agents haven't cleared the building yet," Logan said. "Nobody's going to be allowed inside until they make sure it's safe."

"I—I should stay," she said, hoping to defuse the tense situation between Logan and her brothers, "while they do that."

"But even if the ATF agents declare your place safe," Logan said, "*you're* not."

She shivered.

"You would know," Milek bitterly muttered.

Logan nodded as if in agreement with her brother. Apparently, he hadn't picked up on the deeper meaning. "Neither of us is safe until we catch the person trying to kill us."

Was that why he was acting like her fiancé? Had he decided to use their fake engagement to try to find their would-be killers?

"Us?" Garek snarled the word. "You and Stacy are not an 'us.'" And her brother reached for her, clasping her arm to pull her from Logan's grasp.

Cujo growled in protest, echoing the sound Logan had made low in his throat. His arm tightened around her shoulders, holding her against his side. And the dog stepped in front of him to protect them both from men he had never accepted as alpha males or friends.

"That damn dog likes you?" Milek asked, amused. "That dog doesn't like anybody but Stacy."

"That's not true…" But it absolutely was or at least had been.

Logan reached his free hand down and patted the dog's head. "It's obviously not true," he said. "But then not much of what you guys say is true."

"You self-righteous hypocrite!" Garek stepped closer, but the dog growled louder and bared his teeth completely. So the man stepped back.

"He's not," Stacy defended Logan. She believed that Logan thought he'd been doing the right thing, that he'd been getting justice for his father.

"This is ridiculous," Garek said. "I don't know what's going on between the two of you but it sure isn't love."

Milek studied them through narrowed eyes as if he was beginning to have some doubts that their engagement was fake. Maybe he'd remembered accusing her of having a crush on Logan during their father's trial. "Garek, you're not exactly an expert on love since you've never been in it."

But Milek had? She shrugged off thoughts of her brother's love life. She had enough problems with her own. Life. Not love life. She wasn't in love— no matter what she wanted her brothers to believe.

Garek shuddered. "And I never will be. That's one mistake *I* never intend to make." He turned back toward Stacy with an unspoken plea softening his gaze. "Don't make that mistake either, sis."

He only pulled out *sis* when he really wanted to get to her. It brought her back to when they were kids. And what he and Milek had done to protect her…

"It's too late," she told him. She wasn't in love but she'd committed to Mrs. Payne's plan to protect Logan and to protect her brothers from themselves.

"It is too late," Logan said. "And it's been a long day for Stacy."

"Because of you!" Garek said. "Because *you* crashed our dad's funeral—because *you* put her in danger."

"He didn't put me in danger," Stacy said. But Garek had raised doubts in her mind…and she'd already had enough of those.

"It's been a long day," Logan repeated as if no one else had spoken. "So I'm taking my fiancée home with me."

Garek reached for her arm again until Cujo growled, and he pulled back. "Don't do this, Stace. Don't you dare go anywhere with him!"

But Logan was already leading her toward the SUV parked at the curb. Was her brother right? Was

Logan actually the one who had put her in danger both at the cemetery and at her apartment?

What would happen when she was alone with him? Would he finally exact his revenge? Would he kill her?

Chapter Six

Stacy Kozminski was dead…to the world. She had fallen asleep in Logan's SUV on the way to his house. So after checking to make certain there was no bomb on his kitchen table, he returned to his vehicle, unlocked it and opened the passenger door.

Only Cujo lifted his head from the console. Stacy didn't stir. Her upper body slumped over the seat belt, and her hair had fallen over her face. Fear clutched his heart in a tight fist. Had someone gotten to her without his realizing it? No shot had penetrated the windshield or side glass, though.

And the doors had still been locked. No one had broken inside. They probably wouldn't have dared with Cujo guarding her.

Logan pushed her back against the seat and released the safety belt. Then he brushed her hair off her face and slid his fingers over her throat. Her pulse leaped beneath his fingertips as if she recognized his touch.

Or maybe she'd mistaken him for someone else. For the *friend* who didn't get along with Cujo. *Boyfriend?*

"Good dog," he praised the canine—for protecting her. Then he slid one arm underneath her knees and the other behind her back and lifted her from the seat. Just as she had against the safety belt, she slumped forward—against him. Her face settled into the crook of his neck and shoulder. She murmured and sighed, her breath tickling his throat and causing his skin to heat.

And other parts of his body tensed...

How could this woman affect him like this? They had spent the past fifteen years hating each other... or at least he'd thought he'd hated her.

And not for the reason she and her brothers thought. He didn't blame them for what their father had done. He blamed them for not accepting it and for continuing to support a killer. And he resented her blaming him for her father's sentence and for making certain Patek Kozminski served it. Logan had only wanted justice for his father.

She'd thought he'd wanted vengeance. And she hated him even more than he'd thought he'd hated her. Then she shifted in his arms, burrowing even closer against him—almost into him. But she probably didn't know it was him.

She slept deeply, her heavy breaths steadily whispering against his throat. Even when he shifted her in his arms in order to shoulder open the door to his house, she didn't awaken. Or even murmur again.

Neither did his whistle awaken her when he called for Cujo to jump out of the SUV and join them inside the house. With the dog following closely behind them, Logan passed through the foyer and then the living room, sparing the couch only a glance before dismissing it. It was leather and cold. Even if he'd taken the time to put blankets on it, she deserved better than a couch after the hellish day she'd had.

But he didn't have any guest rooms. The second bedroom of the two-bedroom ranch house held his home office. So he carried her to his bed, which was soft and warm with plaid flannel sheets and a comforter. When he laid her onto the mattress, she hooked her arm around his neck, pulling him down with her.

After the long day he'd had, he should have been as exhausted as she was. He should have been willing to burrow into the blankets like she was and sleep. But if he laid down beside her gorgeous body, the last thing on his mind was going to be sleep. And some damn bodyguard he'd prove to be if he didn't stay awake to protect her from whoever meant her harm.

Harm? The bomb proved whoever was after her didn't want her just hurt; he wanted her dead.

Logan's arms tightened for a moment, holding

her close. He didn't want her dead. He wanted her...
which scared him more than someone shooting at
him. He forced himself to release her and pull away.
But he couldn't get far enough away to stop wanting her—not without compromising her safety.

He had to focus on protecting her. A cold shower
might cool his reaction to having Stacy Kozminski in his house—in his bed. It might also stop his
shoulder from throbbing and force him to think
with his brain instead of another part of his body.

And it wasn't as if he was leaving her unpro-
tected while he showered. She wasn't alone in the
bed any longer. Cujo had climbed onto the mattress
beside her. His furry body was tense and his ears
up and alert for any sound of an intruder.

Eager to be rid of the tuxedo he hated wearing,
he stripped off the jacket and then the shirt and left
them in a trail that led to the master bathroom. But
he held tight to the holster he'd removed with the
shirt and placed his weapon on the granite counter within reach of the shower. He didn't drop his
pants and boxers until he closed the pocket door
and shut out the sight of Stacy sleeping in his bed.

He was too tempted to kick Cujo out of bed
and take his place next to his mistress. His body
throbbed, and it wasn't just his shoulder. A bandage covered the stitches, but he wasn't supposed
to get it wet. He turned on the shower and stepped
beneath the spray before the water had the chance

to warm. It struck his skin like needles, nipping into his sensitive flesh. And he welcomed the pain.

Heck, maybe he was a masochist. Maybe that was why he had become attracted to a woman who hated him. And if he actually agreed to her and his mother's crazy plan to get married, it was destined to end badly. Painfully...

For him.

He glanced down at the bandage on his shoulder. Blood and water saturated the gauze and tape, and the wound beneath the bandage throbbed. But that pain was nothing in comparison to what she could do to him...

Was that why she proposed? To get close enough to him that she could hurt him herself? He should have told her brothers the truth since he doubted it mattered to them whether he was their sister's fiancé. They still wanted him dead. But maybe by posing as her fiancé, he could get close enough to them to find evidence like the gun or get them to confess to the attempts on his life.

A menacing growl emanated from the bedroom. The sound raised more goose bumps on Logan's flesh than the icy water had. He shut off the faucet and listened for whatever Cujo had heard. An engine rumbled in the driveway. And another...

A couple of vehicles had driven up to his house. How many people were after him and Stacy?

He grabbed a towel and hastily wrapped it

around his hips before reaching for his holster and drawing his weapon. He slid open the pocket door to find Cujo standing on his bed, his hair bristling as he stood guard over his mistress. Curled up like a kitten, Stacy was still sleeping soundly.

"Good dog," Logan murmured before slipping from the room to head to the front door and the driveway. Before he reached it, the door opened, so he cocked his gun.

"Don't shoot," his brother said with his hands lifted above his head.

"Then don't sneak up on a man who's been getting shot at," he cautioned Parker. Just in case he might be tempted to use it on his twin, he set his weapon on the butcher-block counter of the island situated between the open kitchen and living-room area. "What are you doing here?"

"It's that whole getting-shot-at thing," Parker said. "I'm checking up on you." He glanced back toward Logan's SUV—he must have closed the passenger door. "Making sure everything's all right…"

If he'd only been acting out of concern as a brother or even out of professional concern as a bodyguard, why hadn't he come alone? Their sister and their top security expert, Candace Baker, had come along with him in their own vehicles. As the women joined Parker inside his house, Logan asked, "What's really going on?"

"You tell us," Parker said.

"I wish I knew," he admitted. He had been so convinced Stacy was behind the attempts on his life. And maybe she was—maybe that was why she'd proposed. Or maybe she'd proposed to save him, as she'd said. But who was going to save her? Because that bomb was proof that he wasn't the only one someone wanted dead...

Parker expelled a ragged sigh of relief. "I knew Mom was messing with us."

"Mom doesn't *mess* with us," Nikki hotly defended her. She had no idea just how manipulative—albeit with good intentions—their mother could be.

Her face tense, Candace curtly explained, "She told us that you're marrying Stacy Kozminski."

He had thought news of the bomb at Stacy's apartment might have brought them here as backup. But now he realized why they'd really shown up.

Parker shook his head. "She's gotta be messing with us. That's the craziest thing I've ever heard."

It was crazy. And Logan couldn't believe his mother's audacity in announcing his fake engagement to everyone. He really should call both her and Stacy liars. A marriage was out of the question. But an engagement...

He might be able to use that to his advantage. "What's so crazy about it?" he asked.

Nikki gasped. "I knew Mom wasn't lying, but I thought she was mistaken. You and Stacy Kozminski…"

"Would kill each other," Parker said. "You can't stand each other!"

"Is that why you guys are here?" he asked. "Is this some kind of intervention?" Maybe he needed one because he was afraid he'd lost his judgment where Stacy was concerned. He found her entirely too attractive…and damn near irresistible.

"Since the definition of an intervention is getting someone to stop doing harm to himself, that's exactly what this is," Candace replied.

"I'm not hurting myself," he said. It wasn't exactly a lie; the cold shower hadn't actually hurt him. That much…

"She will," Candace said. "She's been threatening you for years—every time her father came up for parole she threatened you to not show up."

She'd asked him not to speak at his hearings. She'd even begged once, and while he'd respected how hard that must have been for a woman as proud as she was, he hadn't granted her request. He'd spoken…and maybe his words had influenced the board to deny his parole.

"When her father died after the last hearing, I knew she would make good on her threats. I knew she would try to kill you," Candace said, her face reddening with outrage on his behalf.

She had protected him once from shots fired at him. But Logan had thought then that those shots had been intended for Cooper. Now he knew...

Candace reminded him, "You thought she was the one behind the shootings, too."

Parker's head bobbed in a sharp nod. "That's it. That's why you're doing this—to get evidence against her. It's that whole keep your friends close and your enemies closer..."

After that kiss, he had been tempted to get close to her. Real close.

"Stacy's not my enemy." She wasn't his friend, either, and given their families' histories, they were unlikely to ever become friends.

"Then what is she?" Candace asked, her usually even voice nearly shrill with emotion.

"My fiancée."

While Parker and Candace both sputtered at his announcement, Nikki remained oddly silent. She was usually the most gregarious of the Payne siblings—the most like their mother even though she vehemently denied the comparison. She wanted to be tough and cynical like her brothers. Logan preferred her as she was. Innocent and hopeful and maybe more romantic than she would ever admit. She studied him carefully, as if trying to find something that wasn't there: love.

"Did you let Mom talk you into this?" Parker asked. "Is this one of her matchmaking schemes?"

Probably. "You really think I would let Mom manipulate me into one of her plans?"

"If not, why are you marrying her?" Candace asked. Her voice was still shrill and now he recognized the anger behind it. Why was she so angry about his fake engagement?

Maybe if his siblings had come alone to see him, he would have admitted the truth. But all he really knew about Candace Baker was that she was ex-military and ex-police and now a damn good bodyguard.

He replied in the tone his siblings and employees alike knew brooked no arguments. "I have my reasons."

"Love," Nikki said, as if she'd found what she'd been looking for on his face.

Parker snorted. "Did you hit your head when Logan knocked you down on the church steps earlier? There's no love between him and Stacy. It's called hate."

"It's called passion," Nikki said. "That fine line between love and hate. Those two have been obsessed with each other for years. The way they've stared at each other during court and the parole hearings…"

Candace groaned as if she'd seen it, too.

What had they seen?

Nikki emitted a wistful sigh. "It's so Romeo and Juliet…"

"Yeah," Candace said. "Both of them wound up dead."

Parker chuckled. "Is that one of your reasons, Logan? Love?"

While Nikki continued to study his face, as if waiting for his confirmation, Parker and Candace looked beyond him to the woman who padded barefoot from his bedroom. Instead of her black funeral dress, she wore his tuxedo shirt now with the cuffs rolled up and the tear in the shoulder revealing more of her honey-toned skin. Despite the smudges and blood on the shirt, her black lace bra and panties were visible through the thin white silk.

"Okay," Parker said with an appreciative whistle. "I can see what those reasons are now."

What the hell was Stacy Kozminski up to now? Dressed as she was, the woman was more dangerous than the bomb they'd found in her apartment.

WHAT HAD SHE been thinking? Stacy could have kicked herself for acting so impulsively as to take off her dress and pull on Logan's shirt. She wished that she'd brilliantly planned the action in order to prove the validity of their fake engagement.

But she'd really just acted on impulse. She'd heard that woman's voice—full of jealousy and disdain for her—and she had reacted. Childishly...

Heat flushed her face, but she refused to succumb to humiliation now—especially with that short-haired Amazon woman glaring at her with stark hatred. And jealousy…

Who was she exactly? Did she have a right to that jealousy? What was she to Logan? Stacy had seen her at the last couple of parole hearings, as if she'd come with him to offer her support. Or stick her nose in where it hadn't belonged. Logan had never been married, so she wasn't a current or even an ex-wife.

Girlfriend? Lover? Friend with benefits?

When the woman focused her gaze on him, the hatred left her eyes. Lust and adulation replaced it. "If you're doing this to stop the attempts on your life, it isn't necessary," she told him. "I can protect you—like I've protected you before."

"That won't be necessary," Logan said dismissively.

"You don't think you're in danger any longer?" Parker asked.

"I know that I can protect myself," Logan replied, "I am the CEO of Payne Protection."

With a chuckle of amusement, Parker assured him, "We definitely know you're the boss."

And that woman—that besotted woman—was apparently one of his employees since a family member wouldn't be looking at him like *that*. Like Stacy looked at him…

She couldn't *not* look at him. Except for the bandage on his shoulder, he wore only a towel slung low around his lean hips—his tight buttocks clearly defined, even through the thick terry cloth. His chest and back were bare and broad and all sculpted muscles.

Despite waking up thirsty, she was suddenly nearly drooling. Her skin heated and flushed with attraction. With need…

She had never needed anyone like this before. She had wanted a man before but she'd never *needed* one. Logan Payne was not just any good-looking man. He was the one who had kept her father from her when she'd needed him most. She looked away from Logan's brain-scramblingly sexy body, and her gaze collided with his sister's. Her dark eyes were so much like her mother's—so warm and affectionate. Stacy couldn't recall ever exchanging any words with the youngest Payne before.

Nikki spoke now. "Congratulations," she said as she closed the distance between them and pulled Stacy into a hug.

The woman even felt like her mother—like warmth and safety. But Stacy drew back. "Congratulations?"

"On your engagement," she said with a chuckle. Then she threw her arms around her brother and kissed his cheek. "Congratulations to you, too."

Logan's brows arched; he was apparently as confused as Stacy was over his sister's reaction. The others might have come to stage an intervention, as Stacy had overheard Logan remark, but not Nikki.

"You'll want to get together with Mom soon," Nikki spoke to her again. "Or she'll have your wedding all planned out without any input from you."

Parker and that woman were also looking at Nikki as if she'd lost her mind. But she just smiled and turned for the door. "We should leave them alone now," she said. "They've just gotten engaged."

The woman's face flushed again—with embarrassment and fury—and she turned that gaze of hatred on Stacy. "But Logan's still in danger—probably in even more danger now with her here."

Parker slid an arm around the woman's shoulders and turned her toward the door. "Nikki's right. We should leave them alone." He escorted the women out and then turned back and winked at his twin before he closed the front door behind them all.

Stacy wasn't so certain that leaving them alone was the best idea—especially when Logan turned toward her. His gaze was every bit as intense as his employee's. He was angry with her, but he wasn't just angry. There was passion burning in his bright blue eyes as he stared at her.

Despite the heat of that look, she shivered.

"Maybe you shouldn't have taken off your dress," he suggested. "Then you wouldn't be cold."

She wasn't cold. She was hot. So hot that she lifted trembling fingers to the collar of his shirt.

But she hadn't done up that many buttons so she didn't dare undo any more. "I—I'm fine."

Logan shook his head. "You're lying to me again."

"I haven't lied to you," she said.

"You haven't told me the truth," he said. "Same difference."

"What haven't I told you?"

He shrugged. "If I knew, it wouldn't matter. But I can sense that you're holding something back."

More than he knew. And more than she would ever admit to...

She would touch a bomb before she'd confess to her attraction to him. The bomb was probably less likely to blow up in her face.

She shook her head. "You're paranoid."

"It would be foolish to trust you," he said, "and I'm no fool."

She wished she could say the same, but she had already made a fool out of herself by walking out of the bedroom wearing his shirt. Sure, she could have excused her action as proving their engagement real. But his family wasn't the one they needed to convince; it was hers.

"I know you're up to something," he said, and gestured toward his shirt. But then, his arm outstretched, he hooked a finger inside the collar and pulled her closer. "What are you up to?"

"About five-six," she quipped.

His mouth curved, a grin tugging up the corners of it. "Cute."

"I get that a lot," she said with a smile. God, she was flirting with the man. She was actually flirting. She *never* flirted.

"Your *remark* was cute," he clarified. "Not you."

She sucked in a breath—surprised that even he was insensitive enough to take back his compliment. "Okay, then…"

Since she had really come out wearing his shirt in order to stake her claim on her fake fiancé, she was definitely the fool. She turned back toward the bedroom—and her dress. But he caught her wrist and stopped her.

He stepped close to her so that she felt the heat of his nearly naked body through the thin silk of his shirt. "You're not cute," he repeated.

And she had begun to think that he wasn't as cruel as she'd always believed…

But then he leaned down, his mouth nearly touching her ear, and added, "You're beautiful."

She closed her eyes as pleasure at his compliment radiated throughout her. She wasn't used to compliments. In the past, either she or her brothers had scared off the men who might have been attracted to her. "Now who's up to something?"

"I'm just being honest," he replied. "You might want to try it sometime."

"Honest?" She snorted derisively at his claim of

being honest and his insinuation that she wasn't. "You're just trying to flatter and disarm me."

He turned her around to face him. And seeing his handsome face and all that bare skin rattled her.

She couldn't think. She could barely breathe. Her pulse raced, and her heart beat frantically.

"You are beautiful," he said. "Even when I hated you, I couldn't help but notice that."

"You—you hated me?" She'd known it, but having him outright admit it…caused a twinge of pain in her heart.

Unabashed, he grinned. "You hated me, too. Hell, you still hate me—"

Stacy shook her head. "You saved my life," she said. "I can't hate you anymore." But she wished she could, because with the hatred gone, she couldn't fight the attraction she'd always felt for him.

"You could," he said. "But it would make our marriage a little intense."

Marriage?

Panic squeezed her lungs, stealing away her breath. She couldn't really marry Logan Payne. She opened her mouth to tell him that, but she couldn't get the words out.

Because his mouth covered hers, his lips sliding back and forth across her lips. The friction was sensual and delicious. She gasped at the rush of desire pulsing through her veins.

And he deepened the kiss, sliding his tongue

through her parted lips. She pressed her palms to his chest, but she didn't push him away. Instead, she caressed his skin while she kissed him back.

Their pants for breath mingling, she could taste him. And feel him. His heart beat frantically beneath her palm, matching the crazy rhythm of her own madly pounding heart.

Her knees trembled, like they had earlier, and probably still because of her fear. She was afraid of all these feelings. Afraid that she felt this overwhelming desire—this intense need—for Logan Payne.

Maybe he was just playing games with her, manipulating her with compliments and his mouth and his touch. His hands slid over her back to the curve of her hips, which he clutched, as he dragged her up close to the evidence of his desire for her. He couldn't lie about that.

He wanted her, too. And as if he intended to take her, he swung her up in his arms and headed toward the bedroom. But a low growl stopped him, and his hard body tensed.

"Cujo," she murmured. "It's okay…"

But it really wasn't. Just hours ago Logan had accused her of trying to kill him and now he was kissing her? And worse yet, she was kissing him back. That wasn't okay. It was insanity. But she lied to Cujo because she didn't want the dog attacking Logan.

She didn't want him hurt.

Someone else had another opinion, though, because shots rang out in earsplitting, violent succession. Bullets shattered glass and splintered wood. Shelves and pictures fell from the walls.

Logan fell, too, taking her down with him. The near-dead weight of his long body pressed her into the carpeting of the living-room floor.

Had he been hit again? And this time more critically than his grazed shoulder?

Chapter Seven

Logan cursed himself as much as the shooter. How on earth was he supposed to protect Stacy when he allowed her to distract him so much that someone had been able to drive up to his house without his hearing the vehicle?

Cujo had heard it. But Logan hadn't reacted fast enough to the canine's low growl. And the shots had rung out...

His shoulder stung, but it was from the old wound. No bullets had grazed him this time. Flying glass hadn't even hit *him*.

But he stared down at Stacy. Like in the cemetery, her soft body cushioned his—having taken the brunt of the fall. "Are you all right?" he asked.

Her gray eyes wide with fear, she nodded but flinched as more shots rang out.

"Stay down," he told her even as he rose slightly to ease his weight off her. But he kept his head down as the firing continued.

She clutched at his arms, her fingers digging

into his muscles as she held tightly to him. "You stay down, too." Her eyes widened with more fear. "And Cujo!"

The former K-9 barked at the door, digging at it in his urgency to escape and track down the shooter. But Logan heard the vehicle now, its tires squealing as it spun out of his driveway and back onto the street.

He jumped up and reached for the weapon he'd left on the island counter. But then he had to grab for his slipping towel. It didn't matter now. Even though he ran and threw open the door, he was too late to catch even a glimpse of the vehicle, let alone the shooter.

They'd gotten away. Again. Like every attempt before…

Cujo pushed past him and patrolled the drive, sniffing out probably every dropped shell. How many were they? How many shots had been fired?

It was a wonder neither of them had been hit. Stacy had said she was okay. But was she?

Logan hurried back inside the house. She hadn't moved yet. She was lying on the floor. Still. "Are you really all right?" he asked.

"Are they gone?" she asked.

"Yes," he assured her.

As if she'd been holding it the entire time, her breath shuddered out in a ragged sigh that drew his attention to her breasts. They nearly spilled over the top of her black bra. His shirt had fallen open across that decadent black bra and the matching panties. He groaned in frustration—of his attraction and that the shooter had interrupted them.

Then he tore his gaze from her and looked around his house, assessing the damage. The windows were broken, shattered glass scattered about the hardwood floor. Bullets had knocked pictures and shelves from the walls and penetrated the drywall.

"I should have known better…" he berated himself. Just days ago, Tanya's apartment had been shot up, but those bullets had missed Cooper and the woman who was now his wife. The shots had gone into the ceiling instead of them. Logan and Stacy almost hadn't been as lucky. If Cujo's bark hadn't made him take cover, they would have been hit for sure. "I shouldn't have brought you back here."

Stacy dragged his shirt back together, covering herself as best she could with the thin silk. "No, you shouldn't have," she agreed.

"And I damn well shouldn't have announced it in front of your brothers…" But he'd thought that doing that might actually keep them safe because her brothers wouldn't risk hurting her.

But maybe her family wasn't as close as he'd thought, especially given that someone had planted a bomb inside her apartment.

She vaulted to her feet and pressed her palms

against his chest again. But she wasn't caressing his skin this time. She was shoving him back with such force for her delicate size that she nearly caused him to stumble.

But he held his ground and then he held her, sliding his arms around her trembling body. She struggled against him. "You're wrong! You're so wrong!"

He was. But he was referring to his feelings rather than his suspicions. Even now—even with his house in shambles around them—he wanted her.

He wanted to pick her up again and carry her to his bed, to ignore the damage and the continued threat to his life and hers. But he didn't want to just keep her safe.

He wanted her.

SHE WAS WRONG. She still hated him—because he was so quick to think the worst of the people she loved. And she hated that even though she hated him, she still wanted him. Her skin heated as she pressed her palms against his muscular chest. She intended to push him away, but she was tempted to clutch him close again—to finish what they'd started before the shooting had begun.

Had they actually been about to make love?

No, it would have been just sex; it wouldn't have been making love. There had never been any love lost between them—except for the people they'd loved and lost. Their fathers…

And they would always blame each other for that.

So she forced herself to push back until she broke free of his arms. She stumbled a couple steps before regaining her balance. And, when she averted her gaze from his naked chest and lean hips, she regained her perspective.

"It can't be my brothers," she insisted.

"If you really believed that, you wouldn't have gone along with my mother's crazy plan to marry me," he said. "You know they've been trying to kill me."

"I don't know that," she said. And she'd been wrong, too—more wrong than he'd been—to so easily think the worst of the people she loved. It didn't matter how many times they'd wished him dead instead of their father; that had been just talk. Like the Amazon woman had said, Stacy had uttered her share of threats, too. Empty threats.

He snorted derisively. Maybe he still believed that she'd ordered her brothers to kill him. Or maybe he was just calling her out on the doubts she'd had over her brothers' involvement in those previous shootings.

"They are not the ones who've just shot up your house." She flinched as she took in the damage. She sure as hell hoped it wasn't them. "They know I'm here and they would never risk hurting me," she said. "Not even to hurt you."

"Maybe I'm not the only one they want to hurt," he said. "That bomb was planted in your apartment."

"My brothers had nothing to do with that bomb!" She had absolutely no doubts about that. They might kill *for* her—even if she hadn't asked—but they would never kill her.

"You can't be sure of that," Logan insisted.

"Your brother is the one who knows explosives." And he'd taught Logan enough to be able to stop one from going off. Had he taught him how to make it, too? Had her brothers been right to mistrust him? "And so do you…"

"Cooper shared only a little of his IED knowledge with me," he said. "I disarmed it more with luck than anything else."

She shook her head. "Nobody gets that lucky." At least no one she'd ever known.

"We did," he said. "Both of us. I was there with you."

"Only because I chided you into walking me to my door." She flinched with embarrassment over having done that.

"Chided me?" he asked, his mouth curving into a slight grin.

She clarified, "Threatened to tell your mother that you're not a gentleman."

"She's been told worse things about me," he assured her. "I walked you to your door because I wanted to. And I certainly wouldn't have wanted to if I'd known there was a bomb sitting on your kitchen table."

She believed him. Maybe she was a fool, like her brothers probably thought, to trust him. But she did. "Garek and Milek know nothing about explosives."

"You don't know that," he chided her now. Before she could protest, he added, "Anyone with internet access can learn about explosives."

"So anyone could have set that bomb," she agreed. "Except for my brothers." They weren't killers. *Anymore...* "They didn't shoot up your house, either, so they're not behind the other attempts." *Probably...*

His brow furrowed as if he struggled to follow her logic. He most likely couldn't accept that her brothers were innocent of anything. "Maybe whoever shot at us just now is who set the bomb in your apartment."

He had followed her logic. She breathed a sigh of relief. "And since we agree that's not Milek and Garek, we can break our fake engagement."

"I haven't agreed to anything," he pointed out.

"Logan!" she yelled with frustration at his stubbornness. "I know my brothers would never hurt me. Even *you* have to admit that." But she didn't really expect him to admit to anything—at least not to her.

"That doesn't mean that they haven't shot at *me* before," he said, stubbornly clinging to his suspicions. "I still think they could be behind the attempts on my life."

She shook her head in disbelief. "So you think that someone's trying to kill you—"

"Not someone. Your brothers."

She ignored his accusation and his interruption. "And someone else is trying to kill me? That's ridiculous."

He shrugged off her assessment of his theory. "Why would the same person want both of us dead? What enemy could we possibly share?"

She couldn't believe that she had ever made such an enemy. But she struggled even harder to believe that she shared anything with Logan Payne. She was trying to forget his kisses—but her lips tingled yet with the sensation of his lips sliding over hers.

"I don't know who it could be," she said. "But I know who it's not…"

He sighed in resignation. "Your brothers?"

"And since it's not my brothers," she continued, "there's no reason to continue our engagement, because it obviously didn't dissuade whoever just shot at us."

She waited for the surge of relief. She should be thrilled that her fake engagement was over—that she wouldn't have to pretend to be in love with the man she'd spent the past fifteen years hating. But that surge never came.

"I think it's more likely that there are two different people trying to kill us than that we would actually share an enemy," he said.

She sighed. "You still think my brothers are behind the attempts on your life."

"And you're not entirely sure that I'm not right," he said observantly.

She wasn't.

"So we're still engaged," he said.

"Why?" she asked. "The attempts are still getting made on our lives."

"The engagement gives us an excuse to be together," he said. "And keep each other alive."

"Or wind up killing each other and saving whoever's after us the trouble."

But that *whoever* apparently wasn't patient enough to wait until they killed each other. Cujo, who had never left his position near the front door, began to paw at it again and growl. The shooter or shooters might have returned—probably to find out if any of those bullets they'd fired had struck their target.

"Get in the bedroom," Logan told her.

Her heart pounded furiously but she couldn't stop a smart-aleck comment from coming to her lips—no doubt because of fear and nerves. "How can you think about sex at a time like this?"

He'd drawn his gun from his holster, his nearly naked body all tense and deadly but for the spark of humor her remark had brought to his bright blue eyes. He murmured, "You are going to kill me…"

"If you join me…" But he had a better chance of staying alive than facing the shooter or shooters alone.

He pointed her toward the bedroom. "Take Cujo with you. Go inside and lock the door."

"Cujo won't come with me." She didn't bother calling him, though, because she already knew he would ignore her commands. He was well trained but not strictly for obedience. Like Logan, the canine would always be a cop. The dog kept digging at the outside door, desperate to investigate whatever noise had drawn his attention.

Stacy suspected it was a car's engine but one that had been driven slowly enough that the noise was quiet. Whoever had driven up didn't want to be heard.

"I'm not going to take him outside with me." Logan shook his head. "The old boy's already gotten shot once. He's served his duty."

"You've already gotten shot, too," she reminded him. And she didn't want him getting shot again any more than she wanted Cujo getting shot again.

Logan shrugged his wounded shoulder. "The

bullet barely grazed me." But blood had saturated the bandage, staining it bright red.

"Stay here with me and Cujo," she implored him. "Don't go out there." Because she was afraid that if he did, he might never come back.

But just as she'd known Cujo wouldn't listen to her, she knew that Logan wouldn't, either. Despite having gone into private protection, he was still a cop.

He touched her cheek. "Go into the bedroom and lock the door. And if I don't come back, there's a gun under the bed on the right side. Use it if you need to."

She shook her head. "I don't know how."

"Slide off the safety and shoot," he advised. Then he whistled low, commanding Cujo's attention. The dog turned his head toward them. "Guard her."

Cujo rushed to her side. He'd clearly chosen a new master—someone he would blindly obey.

Stacy didn't blindly obey anyone. "I'll get the gun," she agreed, "but I'm going outside with you. I'll be your backup."

He laughed. "You just admitted you don't know how to shoot a gun."

"And you told me how," she reminded him.

He shook his head. "You're not hired, Ms. Kozminski. You and Cujo need to go to the bedroom." He pointed, and the dog followed his command, nudging her with his big, furry head to push her toward the room. "And only touch that gun as a last resort to protect yourself."

Because he wouldn't be able to...

He was already heading—alone—toward the front door and whatever danger awaited him. He faced and survived danger all the time, so Stacy shouldn't be worried about him. Given their past, she shouldn't worry about him at all.

But she was worried. So worried that she crossed the room, rose up on tiptoe and pressed her lips to his cheek. "Be careful..."

Even as she said it, she knew he wouldn't heed her warning any more than she'd heeded his order. He didn't blindly obey, either.

But he hesitated for just a moment before he turned and opened the door. Then he slipped outside—to whatever danger awaited him....

Chapter Eight

Be careful...

She'd said it as if she cared, as if she was actually worried about him. But she couldn't have been. They weren't really engaged. They weren't really anything...but old enemies.

And almost lovers...

He forced thoughts of her kisses and her nearly naked body from his mind and focused on the vehicle idling in his driveway. Fortunately, he recognized the black Ford Explorer that was a twin to his.

"You plan on ever wearing pants again?" Parker asked from where he leaned against the side of his SUV.

Logan glanced down at the towel he'd forgotten he wore. The terry cloth was dry now.

"I understand why you might be distracted, though," his twin continued.

Logan glanced at his shot-up house. "Yeah..."

"I was talking about your fiancée," Parker said.

"But I'm curious about this, too. That's why I came back when I heard the report of shots fired at your address on my police scanner."

Stacy had accused Logan of still being a cop, but he suspected his twin leaned more toward lawman than bodyguard. At least he'd come back alone... except for the whine of sirens in the distance.

"You should probably find some pants now," Parker remarked. Logan cursed and not just because his brother was always getting on his case, but because Parker wasn't the only one who'd returned. Candace Baker's pickup pulled into the driveway ahead of the police cars. Nikki and his mother would probably show up next. He stalked back into the house.

Just as he'd suspected, Stacy hadn't listened to him, either. She stood in the living room amid the glass and debris. But at least she'd put on her dress again. Without a word, he passed her and headed toward his bedroom and his clothes.

He dressed quickly, and the others were already inside when he walked back out. Cujo stood between them and Stacy, the hair raised on his neck as he uttered a warning growl.

"Good dog," he praised the canine.

"You gonna give him a treat if he bites us?" Parker asked.

"He probably is hungry," Stacy said. "I haven't

had a chance to feed him since we picked him up from the kennel."

"Of course he would be *your* dog," Candace remarked.

His employee's scornful tone had Logan bristling, too. "My mom gave her the dog."

For protection. His mother had thought she needed it. Logan had assumed because of the neighborhood where Stacy lived. But what if his mother had suspected she was in danger for another reason?

He needed to speak to his mom.

"I need to talk to you," Candace said.

The sirens screeched as the police cars pulled into his driveway. "You're not the only one..."

Logan wasn't thrilled about having to take part in another police report. He hadn't liked that part of being a lawman, and he hadn't anticipated taking and giving police reports in his private protection business. And after all the attempts on the lives of his brother Cooper and his bride, Logan had overloaded on police reports.

But now it had gotten even more personal; now he had become a killer's target. But *he* wasn't the only one.

"The police are going to want to talk to you both," Parker said. "I can take Stacy out." He reached out as if to take her arm, but Cujo growled through bared teeth and Parker jerked his arm back.

"Damn dog." He turned toward Logan. "Does he go after you like this?"

Logan chuckled. "No."

"We're twins," Parker said. "You'd think that would fool him."

But clearly the dog knew which of them was which, and he only approved of Logan touching his mistress. Logan was going to have to get the former K-9 officer some special treats.

"I'll go with you," Stacy told his brother as she took his arm.

Logan's stomach muscles clenched with dread. And, he hated to admit, jealousy…

His brother was a notorious playboy. Parker never dated a woman for very long before he moved on to the next conquest. And there was always another conquest. Women were never able to resist Parker.

"I'll go, too," Logan said.

His brother turned back to him, his brows raised in question while his eyes twinkled as if he was fully aware and amused by Logan's jealousy.

"They're going to want to talk to me, too," he explained.

But Candace clutched at his arm, which elicited another growl from Cujo and a warning snarl. She didn't jerk back like Parker had, though.

And Logan had to put his hand on the dog's head to settle him down. "It's okay," he assured his canine protector. But it wasn't…not with his employee holding him back as Parker and Stacy walked outside together—Stacy's small hand on Parker's strong arm.

"Why do you have to talk to me so badly?" he asked Candace. "I'm kind of otherwise occupied…"

"With Stacy Kozminski," she clarified with a snort of disgust. The female bodyguard obviously didn't appreciate his fiancée's attributes as much as Parker did.

He glanced out the shattered window to where his twin stood close to Stacy, his arm actually around her shoulders as she spoke to the police officers. Maybe he was only offering support. But knowing Parker, Logan doubted it and gritted his teeth so that he didn't shout out a protest.

"She's my fiancée," he said through those gritted teeth. Parker probably couldn't hear him, but the words were meant for his twin more than his employee. She shook her head as if in denial of his words.

"You're acting like this engagement is real."

"Why would you think it isn't?" he asked.

"It's like when Cooper married Tanya the first time, as part of the job," she replied. "Just to protect you…or her…"

Cooper had only married Tanya because her real groom had been abducted and she'd needed to marry in order to collect her inheritance. The former marine had said it was for her—for her protection—but he'd also married her because he'd loved her. Always had and always would…

"Cooper and Tanya are definitely real," he reminded her.

She nodded in agreement. "Cooper and Tanya are different. They're in love."

"I'm not talking to you about my love life," he said, and tugged free of her hold on his arm.

"I want to talk about your life," she said. "Being with her is going to put you in danger."

"I was already in danger," he said.

"And you thought she was behind it," she said. "That she told her brothers to try to kill you."

Hearing Candace say his theory aloud made Logan realize how paranoid he'd sounded when he'd accused Stacy of such a horrendous crime. Pushing aside the last of his little, niggling doubts, he admitted, "I thought wrong…"

"No," she said. "You're right. She's done it before. They've killed for her before."

"You don't know the whole story about that…"

"Do you?"

He should have. His mother had tried to tell him, but he'd resented her sympathy for the daughter of his father's killer and had refused to listen. He shook his head in reply to Candace's question, but most of all in disgust at his own single-mindedness. He should have listened to his mother.

He should have learned more about Stacy Kozminski. But he'd hung on so stubbornly to his resentment.

"I know that one man is dead because of her," Candace said. "I don't want you to be the next." Ignoring Cujo's warning growl, she stepped closer to Logan. "Let *me* protect you…"

Her strange tone and urgency had his skin chilling. He'd already told her he could protect himself. Why was she so insistent?

LOGAN'S EMPLOYEE WAS in love with her boss. It was obvious to Stacy. It was obvious to Parker, who watched as Logan and Candace walked out of the shot-up house to talk to the police officers. Logan's twin stared at the female bodyguard with pity. The officers were done questioning Stacy now, but she loathed stepping back inside that house…for all the things that had nearly happened inside it.

They had nearly been shot. And they had nearly made love. Stacy wasn't sure which would have wound up hurting her more.

"How long has she been in love with him?" she asked his twin.

Parker shrugged. "She left the police department to work for him."

"A long time…" She'd even tagged along to those

last two parole hearings. Stacy shivered now as she remembered the woman glaring at her—probably because of the things Stacy had said to Logan. Some not so very pleasant things.

"Yes." Parker sighed now with that pity. "He doesn't know, though."

"What would he do if he knew?" Stacy wondered aloud. Would he act on the woman's feelings? Would he return them?

"He would probably fire her," Parker said. "Which is why none of us has pointed it out to him. She's a damn good bodyguard, and her firing would be a huge loss to Payne Protection."

She nodded in understanding. Parker didn't want her to tell Logan, either. "Why would he fire her, then?"

"Because he would worry that she might lose her perspective." Parker's mouth curved into a slight grin. "He's always adamant about never letting emotions interfere with an assignment."

She laughed.

"Seriously," Parker said. "Logan is a very unemotional guy. Keeps everything inside—never shows his thoughts or feelings."

"Logan?" she repeated, totally shocked at his twin's assessment of the hotheaded, openly judgmental man she knew. "Do you have a triplet? Because you haven't described the man I know."

"You bring out another side of him," Parker said.

"You bring out his emotions." He chuckled now. "That's probably why he's always…" He trailed off, his face flushing with embarrassment over what he'd nearly revealed.

But she knew. "Hated me? Resented me?"

Parker shrugged but didn't deny her comments. "I always thought that it was just about your dad…"

So had she.

"But obviously it was more personal than that. Now I know why he stared at you all the time— he was attracted to you. That probably made him resent you even more." Parker grinned. "I'm glad he finally stopped fighting his feelings."

Hers was the family they needed to fool. Not his. So she opened her mouth to set Parker straight. "It's not what you think," she said. "It's really not…" *Real.*

But before she could finish her confession, a strong arm slid around her shoulders, and Logan pulled her tight against his side. "It's really not what?" he asked. His blue eyes held a warning for her to not admit the truth.

And with the Amazon bodyguard standing behind him, Stacy had no intention of doing any such thing…but sliding her arm around his waist. She felt a twinge of regret that he'd replaced the towel with jeans and a cotton shirt. "Sweetheart," she asked, "are the police done with their report?"

Candace snorted derisively. Over the endearment? Had Logan told her the truth? Stacy doubted that or he wouldn't have stopped her from telling his brother. "It'll take the crime scene techs a while to finish processing…"

She would know since she had once been a cop like Parker and Logan. Before Parker's admission, Stacy had assumed she might have been ex-military like Cooper Payne. She certainly looked the part of a G.I. Jane.

"And it's gonna take a contractor even longer to repair the damage," Parker added. "You're going to need someplace else to stay."

"Maybe the ATF is done with my place," she said. She would like to go home. Alone. But she doubted that Logan was about to leave her side until they figured out who was trying to kill them—since that was the only reason he'd agreed to their fake engagement.

Logan's hand skimmed down her arm to her hip, and he suggestively offered, "We can check into a hotel…"

She shivered in anticipation of what they could do in that hotel. Bad things…

To each other. But mostly bad things for her.

"A hotel won't take Cujo," she reminded him.

As if he'd heard them discussing him, the German shepherd leaped through the opening of the shattered window. They could probably bring him back to the kennel. He would be safer there. But before she could suggest it, the dog rushed to Logan's side.

He patted his head. "Hey, old boy, you've saved our lives a couple of times already. We need him."

"You have other protection," Candace said.

"He'd go crazy in the kennel now," Logan said. "Because he knows we're in danger."

"He's a dog," she murmured disparagingly.

"He's a cop," Logan said in the dog's defense. "He was K-9 before he got shot."

The woman turned toward the dog with new respect. "You're a good boy…"

Her praise didn't woo Cujo any more than it must have Logan. Neither of them paid her any attention as a jangle of metal had them turning to Parker.

He held up a ring of keys. "My place has a fenced yard. The dog would love it."

Logan grabbed the proffered keys and asked, "Where are you going to stay?"

Parker's mouth curved into another grin. "I'm not welcome in my own house?"

"The dog is all I need for backup…"

"The dog can't shoot a gun," Candace said. Obviously she could. She had one holstered beneath her arm like the guys. Could she set a bomb?

Like Logan, she'd thought Stacy was behind the attempts on his life, so she may have decided to get rid of any threat to the man she loved. And if Nikki and Parker were right and Logan had looked at her the way they claimed, maybe the woman had decided to remove the threat to his heart, as well.

Not that Stacy believed she could ever really claim Logan's heart. He would never get over his resentment of her.

"Logan wants to be alone with his fiancée," Parker said, which probably added unnecessary fuel to the woman's already burning resentment. As he had earlier, he hooked his arm around Candace's shoulders and led her toward their vehicles. But then he turned back and said, "Don't worry about me. I'll stay with Mom."

"Sure you wanna risk it?" Logan teased. "Mom's on a roll right now…"

Parker's laugh rang out as he walked away. He stopped at the woman's vehicle first and opened her door for her. The woman didn't appear to appreciate his gentlemanly gesture. She glared at him before sliding beneath the wheel. He slammed the door shut and patted it as if it were a horse he was urging to giddy up. After a few tense moments of staring back at Logan, the woman finally started the engine.

"What is he risking?" Stacy asked. She felt as if she were the one risking everything—alienating her family, making an enemy in the woman who had a crush on Logan and falling for her fake fiancé herself. If it were up to her, she would have preferred to stay with Mrs. Payne than alone with her oldest son.

"He's risking his playboy status." Logan waved at his brother's SUV as the man drove away. Then he pressed his hand to the small of Stacy's back and guided her toward his own vehicle. As his brother had for the bodyguard, Logan opened the door for Stacy.

She climbed into the passenger's seat and asked, "Do you think your mom will talk Parker into a fake engagement, too?"

Logan laughed now. "I don't think even Mom could ever maneuver Parker to the altar." He closed her door and walked around to the driver's side.

Stacy felt as if *she* was the one who'd been maneuvered…into once again being alone with Logan Payne. After he and Cujo jumped inside the SUV, she remarked, "We could have stayed with her."

His handsome face pulled into a tight mask of disapproval. "And put her in the cross fire—again—of whoever's shooting at us?"

"No. Of course not," she said. "I would never want her getting hurt because of me. But you probably think that I have already hurt her…"

He tensed with obvious concern for his mother's safety. "How?"

Stacy paused, surprised that he hadn't immediately agreed with her. "Because of what you think my dad did."

"I *know* that your dad did it," he said, his tension easing only slightly. He turned the key in the ignition, starting up the SUV. "*You* didn't do it. I don't blame you."

Maybe she hadn't heard him correctly over the rumble of the engine. "Yeah, right. You have definitely blamed me and my brothers."

He groaned. "I haven't blamed you for what your dad did. I've blamed you for refusing to admit what he did."

She still refused. "That's because he didn't do it," she insisted. "He never would have pulled the trigger."

"They struggled over the gun."

"He wouldn't have reached for it," she insisted. "My father hates—" a twinge of pain struck her heart as she realized she had to correct herself and use past tense "—hated guns. He never would have touched it."

"It was just the two of them in that room," Logan said. "What do you think happened? How did my father wind up dead and yours not?"

She pointed out what had always been so obvious to her. "There was someone else in that room."

"Officer Cooper didn't see anyone else leaving it," Logan said.

"He wasn't there yet," she said. She had memorized the officer's testimony, and despite fifteen years having passed since the trial, she hadn't forgotten a word. "Your father got to the room first. His partner was slower—too slow to see who really shot your father."

A muscle twitched in Logan's cheek as he turned away from her, his focus on his driving as he steered around the crime scene and police vehicles parked in his driveway. "Your father never said that there was someone else in the room."

Her father had never said anything about what had happened that horrible night. He had chosen to not even testify at his own trial. "I know he wouldn't have done it."

"Then why not tell the police who did?" Logan asked. "He had to have witnessed it."

"I don't know why he wouldn't tell…" Tension throbbed behind her eyes, so she squeezed them shut to relieve some pressure of trying to convince Logan her father was innocent. Why was she even wasting her time? She'd had fifteen years to convince him and had failed. She knew she would never really get through to him. "I don't know…"

Instead of laughing at her or calling her naive as she'd suspected he would, Logan offered an explanation. "Maybe he was protecting someone."

Hope rushed through her, and she opened her eyes to stare at him in shock. "You believe me? You believe my father was innocent?"

He shook his head and dashed her hopes.

If he kept blaming her dad for his father's death,

there was no future for them. That anger and resentment would always remain between them.

Her breath caught with more shock that she had actually hoped there might be a future for them. Had she become such a good actress that she'd convinced herself their engagement could be real?

"I don't know what to believe," he admitted.

"About my father?" He had given her doubts about her brothers; it was only fair that she gave him doubts, too.

"About you," he said. "I thought you were responsible for the attempts on my life, that you'd put your brothers up to it…"

His suspicions chilling her, she shivered. She had been a fool to think there would ever be a future between them. He didn't think the worst of just her family; he thought it of her, too. He always had and that hadn't changed.

Only her feelings had begun to change…

But maybe it was just gratitude that she felt for him since he had saved her life. Twice. But even before that she'd begun to think a little differently about Logan Payne…because of her father's cryptic last words.

"I've been told you've done it before," Logan said. "That you've had your brothers kill for you."

Given the way he'd phrased it, she had a pretty good idea who had told him. The jealous female bodyguard might have bent the truth, but she hadn't outright lied.

So Stacy admitted it. "They have killed for me."

Chapter Nine

Logan hadn't expected her to freely admit it—not when she clung so stubbornly to the illusion of her father's innocence. Stunned by her admission, he'd driven in silence to his brother's house.

"Is this it?" she asked doubtfully as he pulled up to the traditional two-story brick Colonial. "This doesn't look like a place your brother would live…"

"He claims he won it in a poker game," Logan said with a slight chuckle. He suspected his brother used the four-bedroom house to lure women into thinking that he might secretly want a wife and kids someday. But he doubted the playboy Payne would ever wed—no matter how much Mom tried to coerce him into getting married.

She shrugged. "Sometimes I wonder how well we really know our families…"

If she hadn't had doubts about her brothers, she wouldn't have acted on his mother's marriage suggestion. But hearing her actually admit it had disappointment causing a twinge of pain in his chest.

Even while her blind devotion to her father had frustrated him, he'd also admired her loyalty to her family.

"No," she said, as if realizing he'd misconstrued her comments. "That's not what I meant."

"You weren't talking about your brothers?"

Silence was her telling reply.

"You told me earlier that they killed for you before," he reminded her. And he'd been so stunned that he hadn't uttered a single word the entire drive to Parker's house.

Her body bristling with defensiveness, she replied, "I didn't tell them to—"

"But they killed for you."

"To protect me," she said.

He tensed now. "Protect you? Has someone tried to kill you before?"

Her teeth sank so deeply into her bottom lip that she probably almost drew blood, and she shook her head.

So they hadn't killed in order to save her life. What other excuse was there for taking a life? "What were they protecting you from, then?"

She shuddered with such revulsion and horror that he regretted ever bringing up what had obviously been a painful experience for her. As if sensing her pain and feeling it, too, the dog whined and rubbed his head against hers, tousling her streaky blond-brown hair.

"Stacy..." He was going to tell her that she didn't have to tell him, that he didn't need to know. But he realized that he did—that he suddenly needed to know everything there was to know about his fake fiancée.

She drew in a shuddery breath, as if bracing herself, before she continued. "When my father went to prison, we had to go live with my mother again and my—my stepfather."

Outrage coursed through Logan as realization dawned. "Did he..."

She shook her head. "He was trying to...but my brothers broke down the bedroom door. They saved me...but our stepfather died."

If Logan had been the one to break down that door, the bastard wouldn't have survived his wrath, either. For once he respected her brothers. "Which one did it?"

"I don't know," she said. "I blacked out. And when I woke up, they were both hurt badly and he was dead."

"They never told you?"

She shook her head. "It doesn't matter which one of them did it. They both saved me, and they both went to jail for it."

And knowing that cemented Logan's certainty that they would never risk hurting her—not even to protect themselves. They might be trying to kill him, but someone else was trying to kill her. "But if they were both badly beaten, they shouldn't have been charged with anything. It was self-defense."

It had at least been defense—of their sister.

She nodded. "It should have been, but my mother testified otherwise."

"She testified against her own children?" Now he was the one horrified. His mother would have killed the man herself if he'd ever tried to touch one of her children.

"She said that I told them to do it." Her voice cracked with emotion. "Because I was mad that he rejected my advances."

That must have been the twisted story that Candace had learned.

"The jury convicted them of manslaughter," she said, "but the judge believed me over her and gave them light sentences. Milek went to juvenile detention and Garek a minimum security prison for six months."

Neither of those were easy stints. But the jury had convicted them and the judge had probably sentenced them because they'd had previous offenses for stealing, like their father. Could either of them have been with him that night?

But Logan wasn't thinking about that night now. He was thinking about Stacy. "And what about you?" he asked. "Where did you go?"

"I wasn't charged with anything," she said.

"But where did you go?" he asked. "You couldn't have kept living with your mother."

She shuddered again. "No. She signed off her parental rights the day my stepfather died."

"Were you still just fourteen, like you'd been during your father's trial?"

She nodded.

"So you went into the system?"

Her lips curved into a wistful smile. "That might have been better. Because my father asked him, Uncle Iwan let me live with him. But his wife wasn't very gracious about it."

Logan shivered as he remembered the older woman's icy demeanor. "She doesn't seem like the motherly type."

"No. But until I met your mother, I really had no idea what motherly is supposed to be."

She'd obviously had a horrible example of motherhood.

"Your mother is great," she said with more of that wistfulness.

He sighed and agreed, "Yes, she is."

She drove him crazy much of the time—because of her generosity and forgiveness and, most of all, her meddling. But her heart was always in the right place; sometimes it was just too damn big.

Except this time.

He finally understood why his mother had taken such an interest in the daughter of her husband's killer. And he loved her even more for it. His mother. Not Stacy. He didn't love her. But he didn't hate her anymore, either.

"She's great," Stacy repeated. "But she's wrong about the two of us."

Remembering the taste and sensation of Stacy's lips beneath his, Logan's pulse quickened with awareness and attraction and he wasn't so certain that his mother wasn't right about them.

"Her plan isn't working," Stacy continued. "Since our *engagement,* we've nearly been blown up and shot. You really should just take me home. ATF must have cleared my place by now. The building isn't even that big."

The building. "Could the bomb have been meant for the landlord? Maybe someone mistook him for living above the store?"

"The landlord does live above the store," she replied.

He tensed. "You don't live alone?"

"No. I don't."

He'd really misunderstood the situation with her. He'd thought she was as single as he was. But he wasn't just confused. He was disappointed. "Why didn't you say something earlier? The bomb could have been meant for your...*roommate.*"

"My roommate has no enemies." She patted the dog's head. "Cujo is my roommate."

What kind of game was she playing with him? "He's damn well not your landlord, though."

She giggled.

The realization dawned on him. "You own the building," he said.

She nodded. "Me and the bank. Given the property values in that neighborhood, I'm not sure which of us owns more, though."

"And the jewelry store? A tenant?"

She shook her head. "No, it's mine. I design and sell my own jewelry."

That explained the calluses on her hands since she worked with metal and tools and stones. He could have said something about the irony she'd brought up earlier—not only did the daughter of a jewelry thief live above a jewelry store, she owned the jewelry store. But he saw more significance than irony in the situation. "So the bomb could only have been meant for you."

She shook her head again. "I don't know why. I have even fewer enemies than Cujo."

"What about your mother?" Any woman who would testify against her own children…

"She wouldn't have waited fifteen years to exact her revenge," she said with a dismissive shrug. "And she moved on a long time ago and has been married twice since my stepfather died." Her face flushed as if she was embarrassed over her mother's behavior. But she'd felt no shame over her father…

"Now you know why I'm still single," she said.

He wasn't sure if it was because of what had happened with her stepfather or because of her mother's multimarriages. But he nodded.

"You know all my secrets," she said.

"I doubt that."

"You know there's no reason for anyone to want me dead."

"Maybe there's no reason," he allowed. "But someone still wants you dead. Or they damn well wouldn't have planted a bomb in your apartment." He got out the driver's side and walked around the hood to open her door. "So we're staying here tonight."

The sun had dropped low in the sky, the last rays of it shimmering across the asphalt of Parker's street.

"Do you want me to carry you inside again?" he asked. Part of him hoped she did. He liked carrying her, liked the slight weight of her curvy body in his arms, her head on his shoulder…

"No." She sighed and stepped down from the SUV. "It is getting kind of late to go back to my place."

"And yours isn't the safest neighborhood in the daylight," he said. But he didn't intend to let her go home in the morning, either. He didn't intend to let her out of his sight until he figured out who was trying to kill her.

Cujo jumped down from the SUV and followed closely behind his mistress. The dog knew that she was in danger. If only Stacy realized it, too...

SHE WAS IN DANGER. More danger than she'd ever been in before, and she'd had some close calls both in the past and recently. But then her life had been in danger.

Now she was worried about her heart. Why had she told Logan so much about herself? Why had she shared more with him than she ever had with anyone else?

It wasn't as if he was really her fiancé.

He was actually the only enemy she had. But if he was trying to kill her, why did he keep saving her?

In the dim light from the street, he fumbled with Parker's keys before unlocking the door. Cujo pushed past him and crossed the threshold, sniffing his way across the hardwood floor of the living room. Then he bounded up the stairs.

His behavior reminded Stacy of the way he'd acted at her apartment. Her pulse quickened with another kind of fear. "What's he doing?"

The dog's footsteps scratched across the hardwood floors overhead. Logan sighed. "Probably tracking a woman to Parker's bed."

"I'm guessing there've been several," she mused. Was he just following the old scents?

"And several have come back to wait for him."

The dog barked.

"There's a woman in his bed now?" she asked.

"Probably…" But Logan reached for his gun, as if concerned that it might be another kind of threat.

"But the door was locked."

"I'm not the only one he's given his key to," Logan replied. "Usually he gets them back, but sometimes someone makes a copy."

The barking intensified and so did Stacy's fear. "Then he should change his damn locks."

Logan grunted in agreement as he headed toward the stairs. Stacy followed, but he shook his head. "Stay here."

She shook hers in response. She wanted to see what kind of woman would let herself into a man's house and crawl into his bed. And why did an image of herself lying naked in Logan's bed flash through her mind?

Could she be that kind of woman? For him, she was afraid that she could become that desperate, that needy…

She shuddered in apprehension.

"I'm sure it's nothing," Logan said. "Nobody knows we're staying here tonight."

That wasn't true. Parker knew. And more perilously, that jealous Amazon knew.

Could that be who waited in Parker's bed…but for Logan?

She paused midstep, not certain she wanted to see this. But then Cujo growled.

Logan could probably call him off; the dog had recognized him as the alpha male and his master. But Cujo had belonged to Stacy longer. So she continued up the stairs behind Logan.

He moved stealthily down the hall. Stacy tried but, despite being smaller and lighter, she couldn't make her footsteps as quiet as his. The man could have been a jewel thief himself. But he was all about law and order.

And security.

As her father and her brothers had discovered, there was no security in stealing. While her brothers crimes had led to jail time, her father's had led to his death. But then Logan's dad, who'd been all about law and order, too, had also died.

Panic clutched her heart as he stepped through a doorway. His shadow fell back into the hall—dark and foreboding. Had he stepped into a trap?

"Get out of here!" he yelled.

And he wasn't talking to some naked woman in Parker's bed. He was talking to her as she joined him inside the room. While the traditional-looking family home had been misleading about Parker's personality, the bedroom was not. The four-poster king-sized bed and its black satin sheets dominated the space. A black-framed mirror adorned the wall across from the bed and another mirror adorned the ceiling above it.

Maybe that was why Cujo had been barking. Like cats and squirrels and rabbits, he didn't like other dogs, either. Probably because he considered himself a cop instead of a canine.

But Cujo wasn't looking into the mirrors. He was crouched under the bed, growling.

Was the woman under there? Because there was no one in the perfectly made bed.

Logan was crouched down beside the dog, his attention divided between whatever was under there and her. "Get out of here!" he said.

But curiosity overwhelmed her and she leaned down to look, too. Like the bomb on the kitchen table, this one was a tangle of wires and canisters and a clock with flashing numbers. There was time left on this one, though.

Several minutes.

"I can't believe this," she murmured.

"And I can't disarm this one," Logan said with a groan of frustration.

"But you did the other one..."

He shook his head. "This isn't like Cooper described. I don't dare touch it."

She'd rather he didn't try. "We have to leave," she said.

"You go." He slid his gun back into his holster

and pulled out a cell phone. "I'm going to call the bomb squad."

She remembered how long they'd taken to get to her apartment. If Logan hadn't disarmed it, it would have exploded for sure. Like this one would…

"Come with me," she pleaded.

"Go," he told Cujo.

But she hadn't been talking to her dog. She'd been talking to her man. Well, he wasn't her man. And if he blew up, he would never be.

The dog refused to leave Logan's side. And so did she.

"You're only going to distract me," he said. "And I need to pay attention to what the bomb squad is telling me."

She hoped they'd tell him to leave.

"Get out of here," he told her again. "Or all of us will die."

She didn't want any of them to die, him least of all.

"Stacy…" He'd dropped the demanding tone and turned his attention from the bomb to her, his gaze intent and imploring.

She could ignore his orders. But she couldn't deny his wish. Hopefully he couldn't deny hers, either. "Please leave with me," she said. "The house doesn't matter."

"I don't know how much damage this bomb can

do," he said. "It could take out more than this house. It could take out the whole neighborhood."

The suburban neighborhood with all those houses full of families who were probably just finishing up dinner and getting ready for bed.

He handed her his keys. "Take my SUV and drive as far away as you can…"

Before the bomb explodes?

If it did, it wouldn't just take out all those families. It would take out Logan, too.

She didn't want to distract him. But she pressed her lips to his, kissing him deeply. Kissing him as if it were the last time…

SHE WAS GONE, but not so long that his lips weren't still tingling from her kiss. So Logan struggled to concentrate on the instructions coming through the telephone. What if she hadn't gotten far enough away to be out of the danger zone? According to the size of the bomb, that danger zone could encompass multiple blocks.

"Are you sure about this?" a man's voice, sharp with impatience, emanated from the cell phone pressed to Logan's ear. He must have misinterpreted Logan's hesitation for fear. "You can leave and let us handle it when we arrive."

He would like to do nothing better, but he'd found the timer on the device and the numbers were flashing fast. Too fast…

"The minutes are ticking away on this thing," Logan said. And to prove his point of how little time was left he used his cell phone to snap a picture and send it to the ATF number to which dispatch had forwarded his call. He was talking to the captain of the bomb squad, something O'Doyle. "You would never get here in time." Not if the clock was right. He hoped like hell the clock wasn't right. "I'm your only chance."

And that chance was getting slimmer by the second.

"You're taking the biggest chance here, Payne. If this thing blows up in your face…"

He would have no face or anything else left to worry about. But he was more worried about Stacy and her safety. Maybe he should have let her stay. But he hadn't seriously thought she would leave. She hadn't done anything else he'd told her to do.

And maybe she shouldn't have listened to him this time, either. Maybe this was all a ploy to distract him—to get him to not only let her out of his sight but to actually make her leave him.

"How can I be sure this thing is even real?" Logan asked. If he'd been tricked into letting his protective subject out of his sight, Parker would never let him live it down. And if something happened to Stacy, he wasn't sure how he would live… without her.

Even when he'd hated her, she'd constantly been in his thoughts, on his mind.

"I'm studying that picture you snapped me," Captain O'Doyle said, his voice gruff with concern and frustration. "And that thing is not only real but it's incredibly hard to dismantle."

Logan's stomach lurched and he groaned. "Maybe I should just try to evacuate the neighborhood instead." If he drove through the area and blew the horn on his SUV…

No, Stacy had taken his vehicle. Hopefully she'd taken the SUV and was still driving it far, far away.

"There's no time," the captain repeated what Logan had already said. What he already knew.

He drew in a deep breath to steady his nerves and his hands. "Okay, I can do this." Without exhaling, he drew in another breath, swelling his lungs with air and courage. "I can do this…"

Maybe if he said it enough times, he would convince himself and the captain.

"I need you to be completely focused on my instructions, Payne," O'Doyle said, "or you're going to blow yourself up and take most of that neighborhood with you."

Innocent people would lose their lives. And, if she hadn't driven far enough outside the danger zone, Stacy would lose her life, too. So he had to focus, like the captain had warned him. Or he wouldn't be able to protect Stacy or himself.

"Okay," he said. "Tell me what to do. I'm ready…"

To defuse a bomb. Not to die. He wouldn't give whoever was trying to kill him the satisfaction of succeeding. And he didn't want to die before he'd indulged his curiosity—and his inconvenient attraction—to his fake fiancée.

STACY'S HEART BEAT fast and furiously. And her hands trembled so badly that she dropped Logan's keys onto the curb beside the SUV. He wanted her to leave.

He needed her to leave so that he could focus. Knowing that, she picked up the keys and used the fob to unlock the driver's door. Then she slid behind the wheel and fumbled the keys into the ignition. But she didn't have the strength to turn the key.

She couldn't leave Logan to face that kind of danger alone. She would let herself quietly back inside the house; Cujo was so focused on the bomb that he wouldn't give away her presence. She would be quiet. Logan would never know she was there. But she would be there. For him…

Leaving the keys dangling from the ignition, she opened the driver's door to step back onto the curb. But before she could close the door behind herself, strong hands wrapped around her arms.

"You can't make me go," she said. "I'm not leaving you!"

But those weren't Logan's hands on her arms. If they were, her skin would be hot, her pulse racing. Instead, she felt only fear. Fear for him and that bomb he would probably die trying to defuse. And now she felt fear for herself.

Chapter Ten

Lights flashed—on emergency vehicles and on news crews' cameras. Logan squinted against the flashes and peered around, but he couldn't find Stacy. She was gone. He couldn't really blame her. After all, there had been a bomb about to explode that would have, as he'd suspected, taken out most of the neighborhood. His hands shook slightly now, in reaction, but thankfully they'd been steady when he'd needed them to be. Or no one would have been able to identify what might have been left of his body.

"You should consider joining the ATF," the bomb squad captain told him. "You have a knack for this."

"I wouldn't call it a knack," he said. "I'd call it really bad luck."

Clothed all in black with a shaved head, Captain O'Doyle looked like a humorless, no-nonsense kind of man, but he chuckled. "The bad luck would have been if you hadn't disarmed the bombs."

"The bad luck was finding two in one day."

"That is bad luck," the captain agreed. "What's going on with you?"

"I wish I knew..." He'd thought it had been about him—all those shots fired at him. But how could someone have known he would be at his brother's house tonight?

Only Parker and Candace knew...

And whoever might have been milling around the crime scene at his house. Could someone else have blended in with the techs and officers and eavesdropped on their conversation? Maybe they had even seen Parker toss him his house keys?

"What the— What happened here?" Parker asked as he ran up the street from the blockade at the end of it. "My whole neighborhood's been evacuated!"

"This is his house," Logan explained to the captain.

"We have to finish clearing it before we can let your neighbors go back to their homes."

"There are no other explosives," Logan said, and he reached down to pet Cujo's head. The German shepherd leaned heavily against his leg, totally exhausted from his day of saving lives. "This former K-9 cop would have found them. He really has a knack for this."

Captain O'Doyle narrowed his eyes and studied the dog. "We could use him with ATF. You could bring him with you when you join us." One of the other agents called out to him and he headed off.

"ATF?" Parker asked.

"I have a job," Logan reminded him.

"Since you seem to have this whole other calling, I wouldn't mind stepping in as CEO of Payne Protection," Parker said. "It would be a sacrifice, of course…"

"Of course." Logan watched as the bomb squad carried off the undetonated bomb. He held his breath, but it didn't go off in the container as the one at Stacy's apartment had. This had been an entirely different kind of bomb. So, as ATF had told him, it was either a different bomber or a bomber with different signatures. Or two brothers who'd each constructed one of the bombs?

He focused on his own brother again. "But it's a sacrifice you won't need to make."

"I will if you get yourself killed," Parker said. "And right now I'd say my chances of taking over as CEO are pretty good. What's going on?"

Logan shrugged, but his muscles were tense and he grunted at a flash of pain in his wounded shoulder.

"You've been shot at more than once and nearly blown up twice," Parker said.

That wasn't why he was tense.

"Where is she?" he asked, his heart pounding even harder than it had when he'd been disarming the bomb. But then he'd needed to be calm. That was why he'd told her to leave, so worrying about her safety wouldn't distract him. So her closeness wouldn't have his heart pounding as hard and fast as it always did in her presence. "She took my SUV and left. Where is she?"

Parker didn't ask who, he just asked, "She took off?"

"I told her to," Logan explained. "I didn't want her getting hurt. I gave her my keys…"

And he thought she'd taken his SUV and left. But the bomb squad van, which was really the size of a city bus, backed out of the driveway now and revealed the SUV still at the curb where he'd parked it.

"That's not mine," his brother said. "I wasn't allowed onto my own street—let alone anywhere near my driveway."

Logan hurried over to the SUV and reached for the driver's door. It was already open, the dome light shining onto the empty front seats and reflecting off the keys dangling from the ignition.

She had intended to follow his order to drive off, but something—or somebody—had stopped her. He shouted her name, "Stacy!"

"She's not here," Parker stated the obvious. "But she wouldn't have left the SUV and walked off. The way you two are acting—" he narrowed his eyes on Logan's face, as if he questioned if they were only acting "—I doubt she would leave you alone with the bomb. I doubt she'd leave you of her own free will at all."

Apparently Stacy was a better actress than Logan was...because she definitely would have left him. She hadn't wanted to be here with him at all. She'd wanted to go home. But then after they'd discovered the bomb, she had protested leaving him— until he'd insisted—and before she'd left, she'd given him that kiss.

She could have meant that kiss as goodbye forever or as incentive for another hello...

Logan had taken it as incentive.

"Talk to the officer at the barricade," Logan directed his brother. "See if they saw her leaving when they drove up to secure the area."

Parker nodded and hurried back down the street to where the officers and several reporters and other onlookers stood by the barricade. Bulbs flashed and people shouted to him—wanting answers about the evacuation and the presence of the bomb squad. Parker couldn't give anyone answers; he didn't have any himself.

Neither did Logan. Who had set the bomb inside the house? It had been very real, but maybe the person who'd set it hadn't considered it foolproof. And so he'd waited outside to finish off whoever might have escaped the explosion.

Stacy had escaped the bomb, but she hadn't

escaped whoever had taken her right from his vehicle. Had they dragged her off to theirs or was she somewhere in the area?

"Track her," he ordered Cujo. The dog cocked his head as if trying to understand. "Your mistress. Track her." Stacy's scent—her sweet, flowery scent—should be easy for the dog to pick up, Logan figured. He could still smell it—he could smell her—on his clothes and on his skin. The German shepherd lowered his head and sniffed around Logan's truck, and the black-and-tan fur rose and bristled on his neck and back. He hadn't picked up just Stacy's scent; he'd picked up the scent of a stranger, too. The dog followed his nose along the curb and stopped and growled.

Stacy and the stranger's short trail had disappeared—undoubtedly into the back of another vehicle. Logan had been so careful to make certain that nobody had followed them from his house. But then the bomb proved that someone had beaten him there. They must have parked along the street, waiting to make sure the bomb left no survivors.

But Stacy had survived. The bomb.

But was she alive now?

WAS HE ALIVE?

Had he survived the bomb?

Stacy trembled with fear and rage. She leaned forward from the backseat to slam her hand into her brother's shoulder. The car swerved off the winding drive. "How dare you kidnap me!"

"Don't do that!" Garek protested. "Aunt Marta will kill me if I put ruts in her lawn."

Not that Aunt Marta had ever done her own landscaping. She had a grounds crew for that and a house crew to clean the three-story brick mansion to which Garek was driving up.

"And we didn't kidnap you," Milek said, adding his two cents from the shotgun seat.

"You grabbed me off the street like a couple thugs!" she reminded them.

"You were going to run back into a house that you told us had a bomb in it," Milek argued. And they actually hadn't pushed her into their backseat until she'd told them about the bomb. "We couldn't let you risk your life."

"What about Logan?" she asked.

"We don't care about his life," Garek replied. "And for the past fifteen years, neither did you."

"I care," she said. It was no longer a lie. "Take me back there."

Garek shook his head as he turned off the car. "Even if I wanted to, I couldn't," he said. "The police were evacuating the neighborhood as we were leaving."

"Why were you there?" she asked. She would have asked them earlier, but she'd been too furious with them, too furious that they were taking her away from Logan and leaving him alone to face peril.

"We were there to protect you," Milek said.

"Logan is protecting me," she said. Hopefully doing so hadn't cost him his life. Her stomach pitched at the thought—the horror—of Logan dying. Part of that horror was guilt that she had once wished him dead aloud when his statement to the parole board had kept her father in prison.

"He's not doing a very good job of protecting you," Garek complained as he opened the back door for her. He'd locked it earlier so that she hadn't been able to escape the car and run back to Logan and the bomb. "He brought you back to his place which got all shot up. You could've been killed."

"You were there?" she asked.

Had they done the shooting? She hadn't thought they would put her life in danger—not even to take Logan's. That was why she'd proposed to the man she'd always considered an enemy—to keep her brothers from doing something they would regret. Or that she, at least, would regret.

Garek narrowed his eyes and stared at her disapprovingly, like the overprotective big brother he'd always been. "We followed you from your place to *his*."

Logan had told them where he was bringing her. Had they doubted him? Did they doubt their engagement?

"And then you followed us to his brother's?" She hoped they'd followed and not gone ahead to set that bomb. But these were her brothers. They wouldn't risk her life. Would they?

"You didn't ask us if we saw who shot at you at his house," Milek mused. "Why? Did Logan Payne convince you it was us?"

She couldn't deny that he'd tried, but she shook her head. "Did you see anything? At Logan's house? Or at Parker's? Did you see anything suspicious?"

"After we followed you back to Logan's, we left for a while," Milek said with a glance toward the house and the woman who stood in the open doorway.

Following his gaze, she gasped in shock that it wasn't Aunt Marta who stood in the doorway but Mrs. Payne. Aunt Marta and Uncle Iwan stood behind her. Marta looked ready to throw her out while Uncle Iwan just looked as confused as Stacy was.

"I thought you brought me here for an intervention," Stacy said.

Garek laughed. "That would have been a better idea. You must be on something if you're really considering marrying Logan Payne. We should've brought you to rehab instead of bringing you here."

"Why did you bring me here?" she asked...if it hadn't been to talk her out of marrying Logan Payne. But her stomach pitched again as she realized they might not need to talk her out of anything.

She might have already lost her fake fiancé—not to the truth but to a bomb.

Garek gritted his teeth so hard that his words were barely audible as he replied, "We brought you here to plan your wedding."

"Not because we think you should marry this creep," Milek said, his voice low so only she and their brother could hear. "We don't think you should. We don't think you actually will."

"We think you're teaching us a lesson," Garek said. "Or maybe you're teaching him a lesson. Or maybe you're just messing with everyone's heads. But you're not marrying him." He shook his head as if he was trying to convince her—or himself.

"Then why bring me here to plan my wedding?" she asked. Here, of all places. She'd hated living with her aunt and uncle so much that she would have accepted the woman's offer to send her off to boarding school if it wouldn't have been too hard for Stacy to visit her brothers and father in jail.

With a sigh of resignation, Milek replied, "Because she asked us to."

Not Aunt Marta. She would want even less to do with her niece's wedding than Milek and Garek did. Mrs. Payne had asked them, and because Mrs. Payne had asked them, they had obliged her.

Mrs. Payne must not have known about the bomb, or she would have been at Parker's house despite the evacuation order. She would have been there making sure she wouldn't have to plan a funeral rather than a wedding.

Stacy dragged her feet as she approached that open doorway. She didn't want to be the one to tell his mother about the bomb. She didn't want to break a heart that had already been shattered when the woman had lost her husband. But then tires squealed as another car pulled through the gates of the estate, and she turned back toward the black SUV.

Before the vehicle came to a complete stop, Logan threw open the door and jumped out. He was alive! Relief flooded her, weakening her knees as she trembled from the surge.

Garek cursed. "How did he know where to find us?"

The bigger question was how had he survived a bomb? According to him, Cooper had only given him a crash course in improvised explosive devices and he'd gotten lucky last time.

"I told Logan where to meet us, of course," Mrs. Payne said as she joined them on the front steps. Maybe Aunt Marta had thrown her out of her house. "He needs to help plan his wedding."

He wanted nothing to do with a wedding—at least not with a wedding to her. He was going to expose her for the liar that she was. But Stacy didn't care. She didn't care about anything except that he was alive.

STRUCK WITH SUCH FORCE, Logan stumbled back. It was nothing in comparison to what the blast of the bomb might have been had the bomb gone off. But Stacy had nearly exploded off the front steps of her uncle's house as she'd vaulted into his arms. He caught her, his arms closing around her as if they knew she belonged in them. With him…

God, Mom was getting to him with all her brain-washing romance nonsense. Over Stacy's head, he glared at his mother. Why had she come here of all places? And had Garek and Milek bring Stacy here, as well?

One of these people was a killer. Heck, maybe all of these people were killers. Or they would be if one of the bullets had struck, if one of the bombs had exploded.

He held Stacy close to protect her. But he needed to protect his mother, too—from her own optimism. "Mom, it's late. You shouldn't have called this meeting tonight."

She clapped her hands together, and everyone jumped as if another shot had been fired. "There is no time to waste to plan your wedding."

Planning a wedding would be a waste—because the wedding would never take place. She knew that, and that was probably why she was pushing him.

"There's a three-day waiting period for licenses in Michigan," the wedding planner reminded everyone. "But I know a certain judge who might waive that given the circumstances. He did it for your brother."

"Because someone was trying to kill him and his bride," Logan said.

His mother arched a brow. But he didn't need a reminder. He knew someone was trying to kill him and Stacy, too. He could understand one of them trying to murder him—to avenge Patek Kozminski's death.

But her...?

Why would anyone want Stacy dead?

She'd been a pain in his ass, but he didn't want her gone. He just wanted her. Now.

But not as his bride.

"We can't get a license tonight," he said. "It's too late."

"But the judge would meet us down at the courthouse. All he needs is your birth certificate and social security card." She held up an envelope. "I brought yours. And Mrs. Kozminski has Stacy's."

Maybe that was why she'd come here—for that paperwork. Or maybe she wanted to prove to Logan that none of these people wanted him dead. But with the way all the Kozminskis were looking at him, he was lucky that looks couldn't kill. The only Kozminski not looking at him had her face in his chest, her body trembling in his arms. Had she really been that worried about him?

Or was she only trying to sell their fake engagement in order to keep her family from committing murder?

"You—you cannot plan a wedding in three days," Marta Kozminski protested. "That would be impossible."

"I can do it," the wedding planner assured her. "In twenty-four hours…if the judge will waive the waiting period."

"He doesn't need to do that," Logan said.

Stacy tensed in his arms. Maybe she worried that he was going to expose her lie. Her brothers shared a significant look, one almost of triumph.

"I knew it!" Garek said. "I knew it was all bull. You two hate each other's guts. There's no way that you're actually engaged!"

"I don't hate your sister," Logan said.

"Do you love her?" Milek asked.

"Of course he loves her," his mother answered for him. "All these attempts on their lives have forced them to confront their feelings for each other—their love for each other."

Either she was delusional or she really wanted to plan another wedding.

"We realize you're all shocked," Logan said. "We're shocked, too. So we need some time alone to work everything out." He wanted to get Stacy and his mother out of there, far away from all the possible threats.

"So you're not engaged?" the aunt asked hopefully.

Stacy looked at him now, tipping her face up to his. He wanted to kiss her. He *needed* to kiss her. She waited like the others—waited for him to tell the truth and expose their fake engagement.

Chapter Eleven

So Logan lied. "We're engaged."

He wasn't sure it would stop the attempts on their lives, but it would put him in proximity to the suspects to find out which one might be behind the attempts. Of course the Kozminskis hadn't let him or his mother inside their house yet. But as their niece's fiancé, they would eventually have to let him into their family circle. More important, the engagement would also put him in proximity to Stacy. Close proximity. To protect her...

"If you're really engaged, then where's the ring?" Marta challenged them.

Logan spared his mother a glance. She should have known her plan would never work; these people would not be easily fooled. They were used to running the con, not falling for it.

"I—I will design my own, of course," Stacy replied.

"So he's telling the truth?" Marta asked, still skeptical.

Stacy stared at him, surprised that he had actually lied, and nodded.

"Were *you?*" her aunt asked.

Stacy's brow furrowed with confusion and she turned back to the older woman. "What?"

"When you told me that you didn't understand your father's last words?" she asked. "Were you telling the truth then?"

"Dad's last words?" Milek repeated. "What's Aunt Marta talking about?"

Logan was wondering the same. But his mother remained silent, as if she already knew. How close was she to Stacy?

"The warden called her to go to the prison," Garek answered for her. "Dad was asking for her." Was that bitterness or resentment in her brother's voice?

Maybe he and Stacy had been completely wrong about them; maybe they didn't love her as much as either had thought. Maybe that was why the engagement hadn't stopped the shooting or the bombs...

"But he must have died before you got there," Milek said as he reached out to squeeze her shoulder in sympathy. "He was mortally wounded."

She swayed on her legs and leaned heavily against Logan's side. This wasn't easy for her—talking about what must have been a horrific last encounter between her and her dying father. How had Logan not known that she'd been there, that she'd seen the man she'd loved above everyone else die?

"He was alive," she admitted. "But he was barely lucid."

"But he said something to you," Marta Kozminski insisted.

Her brow furrowed again—in irritation as much as confusion. "Whatever my father said to me was between him and me," she said, her voice sharp with anger. "It had nothing to do with *you*."

"It has nothing to do with her," Garek agreed. "But he was our father, too. If he told you something, Milek and I should know what it was."

She shook her head. "It was nothing…"

Marta sneered derisively. "Then you would just say what it was."

Maybe the icy blonde woman was right. If it had been nothing, why wouldn't Stacy just share it? Was whatever her father had told her the reason she was so convinced that he hadn't been alone when his father died? That someone else had been involved?

He wanted to know the truth, too, but he didn't want to press her. She was already trembling with either shock or exhaustion from the eventful day she'd had.

Stacy shook her head. "He was drugged—for the pain. What he said made no sense."

The aunt nodded, as if in acceptance. But then

she sighed. "It is late and my husband and I have no interest in planning a wedding—not so soon after a funeral. It would be in extremely poor taste." She grabbed her husband's arm and tugged him back inside the house and closed the door on them all.

Yet slamming the door on family wasn't poor taste?

Stacy uttered a shaky little sigh of relief. Because they were gone? Or because they'd stopped hounding her about her father's last words?

Her brothers had fallen silent, too. Logan wasn't sure if it was because of the engagement or because of the talk of their father's last moments. The horrific last moments that Stacy alone had witnessed. He tightened his arm around her as her brothers stepped away.

Were they angry with her over the engagement or over her not sharing her father's last words? Logan suspected she was only protecting them.

"We can go back to the chapel," his mother suggested. "And continue the planning."

He shook his head. "We're exhausted, Mom."

"Is that all it is?" she asked, her eyes wide and wet with tears. "Are you mad at me?"

He sighed and eased his arm from around Stacy to put it around his mother. Then he guided her toward her car. Fortunately, the gates were still open; she could drive away. "You shouldn't have come here."

"But I thought it might help…"

His voice low, he said, "It could have gotten you killed."

"None of the Kozminskis would hurt me."

Because they knew she'd already been hurt enough.

"I can't say the same," he said. They all wanted to hurt him. He still wasn't sure that he could trust Stacy. But even if he couldn't trust her, he had to protect her. He was a bodyguard—it wasn't just what he did…it was who he was.

She lifted a slightly trembling hand to pat his cheek as she so often did. "You're my only child that gets mad at me."

A twinge of guilt struck his heart, but he grinned at her words. "I'm the only one who calls you on your crap."

She chuckled. "Yes, you are, my eldest." She pressed a kiss to his cheek and whispered in his ear. "You're going to find out that I'm right about you and Stacy. You're finally going to be happy. That's all I've wanted for you and your brothers and sister."

That was how she justified her meddling—with love. But she was wrong if she thought his and Stacy's engagement had anything to do with love. It had to do with blackmail. Threats. Attraction. Desire…

He closed her door and patted the roof of the car,

urging her to start her engine. He held his breath, not releasing it until her car drove through the gates and away from danger. Then he turned back to the remaining Kozminskis. He wasn't sure who posed the greatest threat to him: the brothers who clearly wanted to kill him or the woman who distracted and attracted him.

Somehow he suspected it was she who would be his downfall.

THE SILENCE WAS even more chilling than the cool night breeze. Stacy shivered. But she didn't break the silence as she and her brothers stared at Logan Payne.

She'd hated him for so long. That hate had kept her strong while she'd worried about her incarcerated dad and her brothers. But the hate was gone now. And she felt weaker and more vulnerable than she'd ever had.

"Tell us the truth," Garek urged her.

"I told you Dad was out of it," she replied. "His last words made no sense." Or so she'd thought at the time. But now she wondered if he might have been right...

"Not about Dad," Garek clarified. "Tell us the truth about this engagement."

"It's not real," Milek said as if trying to convince himself.

After all those years of her very vocal hatred of

Logan Payne, she didn't blame them for doubting that her feelings could have so drastically changed. But when she'd seen him step out of that SUV, she'd felt more than relief and something very far from hatred.

"It's real," Logan answered for her. He wrapped his arm around her, and the warmth of his long, muscular body chased away the chill.

Despite his words, she knew he was lying. It was only real to her. She wasn't sure what it was to him. A joke? A cover to get him close to her family?

"If it's real, why didn't you have your mom rush the marriage license like she wanted?" Milek asked.

"A day or three isn't going to make a difference," he said. "Stacy and I *will* be getting married."

Garek cursed, making his opinion of their union clear. Then he shook his head. "It ain't going to happen."

"Why's that?" Logan asked. "Don't think I'll live to make it to the altar?"

Garek shrugged. "I don't know. But I'd think that eventually your luck'll run out, Payne."

That was Stacy's fear, too. She'd been so scared that he hadn't survived the last bomb. "No," she protested. "It won't run out. We will be getting married."

"Well, until you are, you need to stay with us," Milek said.

Garek nodded in agreement.

She laughed. "When did you two get so old-fashioned?"

"Maybe we've always been," Milek replied. "You just never gave us reason to worry about you before."

"Why are you worried?" she asked. "Because someone's trying to kill me or because I'm engaged to Logan Payne?"

Garek grunted as if he were in physical pain. "Both reasons."

"Then you should be glad she's engaged to me," Logan said. "I'll protect her."

Garek scoffed. "You put her in more danger. She needs to stay far away from you!" He reached out for Stacy's arm.

Cujo wasn't with them, but Logan took his place, snarling, "Don't touch her!"

"She's my sister," Garek said with a snarl of his own.

"She's my fiancée."

"She has a mind and a mouth of her own," Stacy interjected.

"Then tell him," Milek said, "that you're leaving here with us."

She shook her head. Earlier she'd wanted to go home—alone. That was what she'd told Logan when he'd brought her to his brother's house. But after finding that bomb, everything had changed for her.

She was too scared to be alone now. But she wasn't afraid for herself. She was scared—she was terrified—for Logan. She couldn't shoot or defuse bombs, but she wanted to protect Logan. And maybe her presence alone would do that...if her brothers were responsible for the attempts on his life. If they believed she really cared about him, and she stayed close to him, they would stop. They wouldn't risk hurting her.

"I'm leaving here with my fiancé," she told her brothers.

"And don't try to follow us this time," Logan warned them.

"We can't trust you to protect her," Milek said. "You've nearly gotten her shot and blown up."

"He did protect me," Stacy said. "I'm not hurt." But she worried that she would get hurt. Not physically—because Logan wasn't just lucky. He was a talented bodyguard. But she worried that she would get hurt emotionally...because she was starting to believe their engagement was real and that Logan Payne might actually care about her. And that belief would only lead to disappointment. She'd stopped hating him, but she wasn't sure he could stop hating her or her family.

As Logan helped her into the passenger's side of his SUV, he glanced over his shoulder. He couldn't believe that her brothers hadn't tried to stop them again—that they had just let them walk away. But Stacy had made it clear that she was leaving with him.

Why?

He stared into her face and noticed how her gray eyes darkened with fear. She was afraid. "Don't worry," he reassured her. "I'm taking you to one of the safe houses I use for clients in danger."

Which was where he should have taken her when he'd first found that bomb in her apartment—instead of to his place and then to Parker's. But he'd been so certain that her brothers were responsible that he'd been convinced the attempts would stop when she was near him.

Either he was wrong about them or she was. Maybe they didn't care as much about her as either of them had thought.

She tensed as if something had just occurred to her and asked, "Where's Cujo? I thought you'd left him in your car. He didn't get hurt—"

"No," Logan told her. "I brought him back to the kennel where we picked him up. I thought he'd had enough excitement for one day."

She nodded. "Of course. But we can pick him up now."

He wasn't convinced the excitement was over. "It's late," he reminded her. "We'll have to wait until morning."

Which was probably only a few hours from now.

He closed her door and walked around the front to the driver's side.

Like thugs on a street corner eyeing a potential victim, her brothers watched him. The weight of the gun in the holster beneath his arm reassured him. But he didn't want to shoot one of Stacy's brothers. She would already probably never forgive him for her father dying in prison, but if he had to kill one of her brothers, too…

He had been so positive that they were responsible for the attempts on his life. But now he hoped they weren't. He hoped it was anyone else.

But who? And why would that person be after both him and Stacy?

He opened the driver's door and slid beneath the wheel. The dome light illuminated Stacy's pale face. The only color to her blanched skin was the dark circles beneath her eyes. She was exhausted. It hadn't just been one long emotional day but a few days for her.

"I'll keep you safe," he promised in case her brothers had put any doubts in her mind. But then the bomb had probably done that.

"I know."

Did she really? Did she trust him?

He felt the weight of that trust more heavily than his weapon. He would keep her safe, or he would die trying.

She must have really trusted him because she

lay back and closed her eyes. So she didn't see the lights behind them.

But he saw them and cursed.

Her body tensed, and her eyes opened. She hadn't been asleep at all. "What?"

"Your brothers must be following us again." At least this time he'd noticed them. How had he missed their tail before?

"They want to protect me," she said.

He wasn't so certain that was their real purpose in following them. But then he didn't blame them for not trusting him with her safety. But because he suspected them, he sped up to lose them.

"I'll protect you," he said.

"Why?" she asked.

"I'm a bodyguard," he reminded her. "It's what I do." He made a couple quick turns, and the road darkened behind them. He'd lost the tail. That easily?

Too easily...

He pressed harder on the accelerator and squealed around a few more sharp turns.

Stacy braced her hands on the dashboard. "But why protect me?" she asked. "I didn't hire you."

"You didn't need to," he said. On some level he felt as if he owed her. Keeping her father in prison had been the right thing—the just thing—but it had also hurt her. The road remained dark behind them. At this hour, theirs was the only car on the road.

"Why did you lie to my family about the engagement?" she asked.

He shrugged. Maybe his mother had gotten to him—not with her matchmaking, but with her suggestion that a marriage between him and Stacy would stop the attempts on his life. The engagement hadn't. But that might have made her brothers even more determined to kill him before he could marry their sister. The engagement might have put him in even more danger.

"Maybe I wasn't lying," he said. "Maybe we should make it real."

The lights flashed behind him again—the beams on bright—as the car roared up behind them. "Your brothers…"

She turned toward the lights and then jerked forward, her head dangerously close to the dashboard, as the car slammed into the back bumper of his SUV.

"That's not my brothers," she protested, her voice cracking with fear. "That's someone trying to kill us."

The car must have been bigger than it looked, because as it slammed into them again, the SUV swerved, nearly sliding off the road.

Stacy screamed, and Logan cursed. He'd promised to protect her. And he intended to keep that promise. But that driver wasn't just trying to kill them; he was *determined* to kill them.

Chapter Twelve

Maybe we should make it real...

Stacy had never gotten the chance to ask Logan what he'd meant before all hell had broken loose. She braced her hands on the dashboard as the car struck them again with such force that the SUV swerved off the road. It spun around, and her head struck the post next to her seat between the passenger side doors.

She screamed again as fear overwhelmed her.

Spots danced before her eyes, her vision blurring. She blinked to clear her mind—to focus—but her ears rang from the impact of hitting her head.

Gravel flew up behind them, pinging off the metal. Logan steered between trees. Metal crunched now as the side mirror twisted off and broke. Then he was back on the road, behind the car—his lights shining into the vehicle and illuminating two shadows.

"Are you okay?" he asked her, his voice gruff with concern. "Stacy!"

The urgency in his voice jolted her. "I'm okay," she said, even as her head throbbed with pain and her heart with fear. "Are you?"

"Oh, yeah," he said. Excitement replaced his concern as he sped up. The pursued had become the pursuer. He struck the rear bumper of the car.

The gunfire hadn't killed them, neither had those two bombs, but his driving might. He cursed, then sighed. "I can't…"

Was the car faster?

"Why not?" she asked. She wanted this person stopped—wanted this all to be over.

"They probably have guns."

So he braked and spun the SUV around, going the other direction. Stacy braced her hands against the dashboard as he careened around corners, taking an on-ramp well over the posted speed. They were on the freeway only moments before he crossed four lanes to an off-ramp. The car tires squealed as he careened around that sharp turn.

Feeling sick, she turned toward him and noticed a slight grin on his lips. "You're enjoying this," she accused him.

How was that possible when she had never been so scared? Except maybe when they'd found the bomb or been shot at…

"The driving, yes," he admitted.

He was quite the expert driver. He'd handled the other car slamming into them, and he'd certainly lost that car now. There were no headlights behind them. Not even any taillights ahead of them.

"I haven't enjoyed getting shot at or defusing bombs." The grin left his face, replaced by a tension that had a muscle twitching in his cheek. "I haven't enjoyed any of that."

"I haven't," she said. "But I thought you would be used to getting shot at and nearly blown up...what with being a bodyguard now and a cop before that."

He sighed. "Just because I'm used to it doesn't mean I enjoy it."

"Then why do you do it?" she asked. "Why would you go into private security?"

"To keep people safe," he said.

"Then why didn't you stay a police officer?" she wondered. "They keep people safe."

He shook his head. "No. They don't."

Was he thinking again of Robert Cooper, of the cop who hadn't protected his partner, Logan's father?

"The police show up *after* the fact," he said. "*After* someone's violated the restraining order or after a stalker crosses the line to violence."

"You saw a lot of horrible things while you were with the River City Police Department," she realized. And because he had been too late to help those victims and probably because he'd been unable to save his father, too, he'd gone into private protection.

"What you saw would have been worse," he said. He reached across the console for her hand, intertwining their fingers. "When you went to the prison infirmary."

She shuddered at the memory of her father in so much pain and the awful helplessness she'd felt. "I wish I'd been able to do something for him…"

"The doctors weren't able to save him," he said. "There was nothing you could do. I'm surprised he would even want you to see him like that."

Apparently even Logan had known that her father had always tried to protect her. And maybe that was what his last words had been about…

"Whatever he'd wanted to tell you must have been really important," he said, his deep voice rising slightly as if in a question.

It hadn't seemed that important at the time he'd said it. In fact, she hadn't understood him at all. Until now…until she'd become Logan Payne's fake fiancée.

Maybe we should make it real…

Did he actually want to marry her?

"What did he say to you?" Logan persisted.

She uttered a weary sigh. "Like I told my family, I don't want to talk about it. I'm exhausted…"

He squeezed her fingers. "I'm sorry."

Guilt flashed through her. She had lied to put him off as she had everyone else. But then she realized she wasn't lying. She was completely exhausted, so exhausted that she settled against the seat and closed her eyes. She didn't notice his driving or the danger anymore. With his hand holding hers, she felt safe—truly protected for perhaps the first time in her life, and sleep claimed her.

EVEN THOUGH HE'D driven like a madman, Logan had been careful. No one could have followed him this time. But then he hadn't thought he'd been followed before...until the Kozminskis had. Had her brothers been in the vehicle that had tried to force them off the road? Or was she right? Had it been someone else?

Just like he'd steered it between trees, he steered the SUV through a narrow garage door built into the basement of the safe house where he'd brought his fiancée. Was it fake anymore? Or should she become his bride?

She murmured in her sleep, drawing his attention. Not that she'd ever *not* had it. Even when he'd been watching the rearview mirror for any sign of someone following them again, he had been aware of her sleeping in the seat next to him. She hadn't been lying about being exhausted.

Even now she barely stirred as he reached over and unbuckled her belt. Like he had earlier that day—or yesterday, actually—he carried her into the house. But this wasn't his house.

He'd brought her to a lakefront condo that a

grateful client let Logan use when he, the owner, was in Florida. The town house was one of several in a converted piano factory. He had to shift Stacy in his arms so that he could operate the wooden elevator to carry them to the upper floors from the basement garage.

Her head slid into the cradle of his neck and shoulder, and her lips brushed across his throat. His heart raced.

He should have been exhausted, too. It hadn't just been a long day. Because of the danger his brother and his bride had been in, it had been a long week with little sleep and too many rushes of adrenaline.

But this—holding Stacy in his arms and, earlier, kissing her—was a bigger rush than defusing bombs or dodging bullets or evading vehicles. But she wasn't awake...

"Sorry," she murmured sleepily, her breath warm against his ear.

He cleared his throat. "Sorry?"

"Sorry you have to keep carrying me." She wriggled in his arms until he loosened his grasp enough that she slid down his body.

"I don't mind," he said. He actually enjoyed it, enjoyed taking care of a woman who was usually so fiercely independent and strong. "I know you're exhausted."

"You must be, too."

He shook his head. "No, not so tired anymore."

The elevator ground to a halt on the top floor—
the bedroom loft. Now he wasn't tired at all. He
slid open the wooden accordion door. She started
across and stumbled on the uneven threshold and
fell back against him. He caught her up in his arms
again and carried her to the bed.

"You don't need to do this," she protested.

"Maybe I want to do this," he said as he lowered her to the mattress, which was on a bamboo
platform with pillows piled up against the exposed
brick wall.

He wanted to join her in the bed. But he forced
himself to release her and step back.

"You do?" she asked.

"I want to keep you safe," he said. And if he intended to do that, he needed to control his urges.
He wanted her—badly—so badly that he wouldn't
be tender and gentle. And she was too tired—physically and emotionally—and too vulnerable to deal
with his desires.

"Where are we?" she asked as she peered around
at the brick and exposed ductwork and beams and
the scarred hardwood floors.

"A safe place."

"You're not going to tell me where," she surmised. "I wouldn't tell anyone where we are, you
know."

"I know," he said. "You're good at keeping secrets." He doubted she would tell him what her

father's last words had been, but there might be another way he could find out. "This condo belongs to a friend…"

She glanced around again at all the dark woods and fabrics. "It's not a female friend, right? It doesn't belong to that Amazon who works for you?"

He shook his head, confused by the sharpness of her tone. "No."

"You didn't tell her where we are?"

"I didn't tell anyone," he assured her. "We're safe. But we would've been safe if Candace knew where we are, too."

She chuckled. "You would be. But not me."

"What do you mean?"

"How can you be so observant and not realize how she feels about you?" she asked.

"What do you mean?"

"She's in love with you," Stacy said. "She's obsessed with you. And she must've considered me a threat—even before our fake engagement. She went to the last couple of parole hearings with you."

Maybe he was more tired than he'd thought because she wasn't making any sense to him. Candace was in love with him? "What are you saying?"

"It could have been her shooting at us earlier," she suggested. "It could have been her who set the bomb. She was one of the few who knew we were going to Parker's."

That was true. But in love with him?

Then he remembered how she'd acted about the engagement announcement. She hadn't just been concerned. She'd acted almost jealous. But even if she had feelings for him, she wouldn't have tried to kill Stacy. Or him.

Candace had been a cop, too; she had sworn to protect and serve. She would never endanger anyone. "No."

Or would she? She had been acting strangely.

"You would rather think it was my family," Stacy accused him.

"I would," he admitted. Because if it wasn't, then he had been wrong about everyone, and he had always prided himself on being a good judge of character.

Her weariness was back and her shoulders slumped as if she was defeated. "At least you're being honest with me."

"You're tired," he said. "Go back to sleep."

She stood up next to the bed and turned to look at it as if considering. "Is there only one bed?"

"Don't worry," he said. "It's yours." Then he chuckled. "Apparently, your brothers aren't the only old-fashioned ones in your family."

Her eyes flashed at him with annoyance. "I'm not old-fashioned." And as if to prove it, she reached for the zipper at the back of her dress.

She was going to undress in front of him?

His heart slammed into his ribs. But the dress didn't come off. The zipper didn't even come down.

She bit her lip as she continued to tug. "It's stuck."

"Let me help you," he said. Gripping her shoulders, he turned her back to him. Then he pushed aside the heavy tangle of her tawny-colored hair and fumbled with the zipper of her black dress.

"It's stuck," she said.

Fabric was caught in it. She would have dressed quickly back at his house—after the shooting and before the police arrived—so quickly that she'd caught the fabric. He pulled it loose. Then he swallowed hard before pulling down the tab. Metal zipped as the teeth separated, baring a strip of skin that looked silky. That strip revealed the curve of her spine and the dimples at the base of it—on the rise of her butt.

His heart beat erratically—as if it were stopping and starting. He drew in an unsteady breath as the dress fell, sliding down her body.

He'd seen her in the black bra and panties earlier when she'd worn his shirt over them to flaunt their fake engagement. They were engaged. But they weren't really together despite what they'd nearly done earlier, before someone had shot up his house.

But the two of them probably would have stopped—even without the gunfire. Too much history and pain separated them. He wanted to close the distance between them. But he forced himself to step back again.

"I'm...uh...I'm going to shower," he said. And hopefully the water would be icy enough to cool the heat of his desire for her.

She turned toward him and stood there in just that black bra and panties. Maybe she was so tired she was befuddled, because she looked confused. And vulnerable.

The vulnerability steeled his control. He could not take advantage of that vulnerability.

He backed away until he stepped through the doorway to the master bath. Then he closed that door between them. Like the rest of the town house, it was all brick, dark wood and shiny steel. He set his steel—his holstered gun—onto the counter along with his cell phone. Then he shucked off his jeans and the cotton shirt, which fortunately bore no bullet holes. He dropped it onto the floor along with his boxers.

Then he turned on the shower and stepped beneath the blast of cold water. The water pressure was forceful and loud—but not so loud that he didn't hear the telltale creak of the door opening.

He had been so certain that he'd lost that car that had tried driving them off the road. He'd been so certain that they would be safe here...

But Stacy wouldn't have followed him into the bathroom. She had looked so exhausted that she'd probably dropped onto the bed and fallen immediately back to sleep. So someone else must have gotten inside the town house.

His heart beat heavy with dread and fear. They would have gotten to Stacy already.

Could he get to his gun before they got to him?

Chapter Thirteen

Strong, wet arms wrapped tightly around Stacy, lifting her off her feet and whirling her around to face a naked, mad Logan Payne.

"What are you doing?" he asked.

That was a damn good question—one she should have asked herself before she'd followed him into the bathroom. But that look on his face—that look she'd mistaken for longing and desire—had drawn her after him.

That look was replaced with anger now. "You shouldn't sneak up on me. I could have hurt you."

He would hurt her. Eventually. She was certain of it because she was beginning to have feelings for her fake fiancé. And he obviously didn't return those feelings.

"Why'd you come in here?" he asked. "Did you need to use the bathroom?"

"I—I…I needed…" Him. She'd needed her fiancé. Her face heated with embarrassment over that need, but she couldn't admit it now, not in the face of his anger.

"What do you need?" he asked her. He stood before her gloriously naked, and she couldn't help but stare, her gaze skimming hungrily over every slick, muscular inch of him. As she watched, his body grew hard and tense. His voice gruff with desire, he asked again, "What do you want?"

She'd been keeping secrets from him. But she couldn't lie about her feelings anymore. "You," she replied. "I want you. I need you."

He carried her again, but this time she didn't protest. Her skin heated everywhere his skin touched. And then instead of just laying her down on the bed, he followed her down—his body covering hers while his mouth covered hers.

He kissed her passionately, as if he was as hungry for her as she was for him. His lips pressed against hers and his tongue delved inside her mouth, making love to it, like she wanted him to make love to her body.

She'd never felt such passion. Such need. Her arms clasped his back, her fingers skimming down his spine to his tight butt. She pulled him against her arching hips. His erection hardened and pulsed against her.

He groaned. "Stacy, slow down…"

She nearly giggled. That was something she'd never been told before. Usually she was told that she went too slow, that she was too cautious. Even he had accused her of being old-fashioned and the comment had stung because it was true. That was why there had been so few men in her life and even fewer in her bed.

He leaned his forehead against hers and drew in deep breaths. But she could feel his heart racing against hers. He wanted her as much as she wanted him.

"Why?" she asked. "Why do I have to slow down?"

He kissed her lips again but it was a light, gentle kiss. "So we can make it last. So I can last…"

"It's okay if you don't," she assured him.

He shook his head. "No, it's not. I want you to enjoy this," he said, "every bit as much as I intend to."

She was enjoying it—every soft kiss. He moved from her lips to her chin and then down her throat. He flicked his tongue across her leaping pulse point. Then he nibbled on her collarbone.

While he'd told her to slow down, the man moved fast, removing her bra and panties before she even realized they were gone. She realized when he touched her there—first with his fingers tracing over the curves of her breasts before teasing the nipples. One hand moved lower, over her stomach to the small mound between her legs.

She squirmed beneath him as pressure built

inside her. While his hands stroked her breasts and lower, his lips moved back to hers. The gentle kisses were gone as he kissed her more forcefully now.

Her hold on reality began to slip as he drove her crazy with those kisses and caresses. And she wanted him to descend to madness with her, so she touched him, too. She skimmed her palms over his muscular chest and down his stomach until she could encircle him with her hands. It took both and still he protruded over the top.

He groaned into her mouth. "Stacy…"

"I'm not slowing down now," she protested. Not when the pressure building inside her was about to snap her in two. He stroked her again—deep—and she peaked. Panting for breath, she arched against him. But she wanted more than his touch. She wanted all of him, so she guided his erection inside her.

He thrust, sliding in and out of her, driving her to the brink of madness again as passion overwhelmed her. She'd never felt anything like this—such an intensity of desire and pleasure.

And such intimacy…

With him inside her, she felt so close to him—closer than she'd ever felt to another human being. He kept his mouth on hers, kissing her as deeply as he was driving inside her. And he kept touching her, running his hands all over her body as if he were trying to memorize every inch of her flesh.

She kept touching him, too, unable to stop touching him, unable to stop moving beneath him. She squirmed and arched. Then he reached between them and rubbed his thumb against the most sensitive part of her, and pleasure overwhelmed her again. She screamed his name as her body shook and shuddered with an orgasm more intense than any she'd ever felt before.

With a guttural groan of pleasure, he joined her, his orgasm filling her. He settled his forehead against hers and stared deeply into her eyes.

And she hoped that he didn't see what that had meant to her. *Everything*.

She had just made love to the man she'd spent the past fifteen years hating. If lying about being engaged to him was a betrayal of her family, this was worse. Making love with him was a betrayal of herself...

"This was a mistake," she murmured.

He sucked in a breath as if she'd struck him. "I thought you wanted it."

"I did," she said. And she did again—even though he was still inside her. She wanted him. "But it complicates everything."

"Everything wasn't already complicated?" he asked. "With people trying to kill us?"

"I was thinking more of our history," she said. Their complicated history of hating each other.

And finally he pulled out of her.

She felt empty—more empty and alone than she'd ever felt, even when her father and brothers had been *away*.

He uttered a ragged sigh. "That's right. You hate me."

"Ah, hell," she murmured as she pushed him back onto the mattress. "I don't hate you. I wish I hated you…" But she was afraid that she was falling for him instead. She swung one leg across his lean hips to straddle him. "I want you…"

His hands caught her hips, his fingers digging into the flesh of her butt as he stilled her. Had she reminded him that he hated her?

"I'm going to need a minute to recover."

He lied. It didn't take him a full minute to recover. It took him much longer to reach his pleasure breaking point, though. So she was able to enjoy herself—setting her own pace as she slid up and down him and rocked back and forth.

Sweat beaded on his upper lip and the muscles in his arms and neck corded and pulsed. He waited until she peaked again, and then he thrust up, hard, and joined her in ecstasy.

She dropped onto his chest, so exhausted that she was boneless with sexual satisfaction. She'd never been so fulfilled or so exhausted. Feeling safe and secure in his arms, she easily fell asleep.

LOGAN SHOULD HAVE been tired. Exhausted now. But he couldn't close his eyes. He could not take his gaze off her. He watched as the bright sunshine of midmorning streaked through the bedroom blinds and fell across Stacy's face, illuminating her already luminous beauty.

He would like to blame his inability to sleep on his having to stand watch and protect her. But he had made certain that no one had followed them here. And nobody knew where he'd brought her. He hadn't even told Parker.

Not that he told Parker everything. Despite being twins, they didn't have that intuitive connection that twins were rumored to have. They didn't tell each other everything. Parker had his secrets— about women. Logan suspected he'd slept with a few of their female clients, which was an offense that merited termination from the Payne Protection Agency. So of course he wouldn't have admitted to the boss what or whom he'd done.

But Logan kept his secrets, too—about women. He wouldn't admit to his feelings for his fiancée to his twin. He wasn't even ready to admit to those feelings to himself. For so long he'd thought he'd hated Stacy Kozminski. When they'd made love, his feelings had been intense—more intense than anything he'd felt before. He definitely didn't hate her.

But he didn't want to love her, either…because nobody kept more secrets than Stacy Kozminski. And he couldn't love someone he couldn't trust.

A phone rang, shattering the silence of the town house and scattering Logan's thoughts. Beside him, Stacy tensed and jerked awake. In a fearful whisper she asked, "Who knows we're here?"

"Nobody," he soothed her. And that was probably why someone was calling—to find out where the hell he was. "That's not the landline. It's my cell."

He'd left it on the bathroom counter with his gun. So he had to leave her to answer it. He had to unwrap his arms from around her warm, nude body. Then he had to slide across the bed. Cold air rushed over him, chilling his naked skin as he padded into the bathroom and grabbed his phone.

If it was Parker…

But it wasn't Parker's number on the caller ID. He answered, "Logan Payne."

"Payne, Captain O'Doyle here."

He'd recognized the number; it wasn't one he was ever likely to forget, but one he hoped he would never have to use again. "Captain, I didn't think you were serious about that job offer—at least not serious enough to call so soon."

"It's nearly noon, Payne," the captain replied

with a chuckle. "I didn't think I'd be waking you up at noon."

"You didn't wake me." And it was noon? How had he stayed awake all night?

"Too much adrenaline to sleep," the captain replied. "That usually happens after defusing a monster like that bomb."

It wasn't the bomb that had had adrenaline rushing through his body. It was Stacy.

"And I was serious about that job offer," O'Doyle continued. "But that's not why I called. I got back the initial report on the bomb."

"The monster?"

"No, that one's pretty professional."

"The first one wasn't?"

"No. It was crude and amateurish. If it's the same bomber, he's a fast learner and vastly improved for his second attempt."

"When I was back on the force, whenever we were chasing a serial killer, we wanted to find his first kill because that was the one he would have made his mistakes on…"

The captain chuckled. "You are good, Payne. You're wasted on private security."

He glanced through the open door to where Stacy had fallen back to sleep in the bed—her beautiful face and naked body completely bathed in sunshine now. "No. Not wasted at all."

Not as long as he could keep her safe.

"So what did you find on the first bomb?" he asked.

"We learned that the components to buy it were stolen from a hardware store just down the block from the jewelry store."

"Were there cameras? Witnesses?"

"No cameras, and it happened after the place closed. No one sees anything in that neighborhood, you know."

"Of course not."

"But we know what day the store was broken into."

And when the captain named the day, Logan's blood chilled. It was the same day that Stacy's father had died in prison. Why had someone chosen that day to make the bomb and set it in Stacy's apartment?

Because of her father's last words? The words she'd refused to share with anyone else—even with her family?

"I thought you'd be more excited about the news," O'Doyle said.

"I'd be more excited if we knew who actually made the bomb."

The ATF agent chuckled. "Thought you'd want me to leave some work for you to do. Let me know if you figure it out…"

"When," Logan corrected him. "I'll let you know *when* I figure it out." Because it had just occurred to him how he might do that.

He hung up on the ATF agent and returned to the bed where Stacy slept. But he didn't join her on the soft mattress and the silk sheets. He just stood over her, watching her sleep as he must have most of the morning.

He wanted to keep her here—in this private town house where nobody knew where they were. He wanted to keep her safe. But she would only be truly safe when the threat against them was eliminated.

"Stacy…"

She didn't stir.

"Stacy!"

She jerked awake like she had when the phone rang. "What? What's wrong?"

Everything.

"You have to get up," he said. "You have to get dressed."

"Why?" she asked. "Why are we leaving? Does someone know we're here?"

"Nobody does," he assured her.

"Then why can't we stay?"

He wished they could. He wished they could just pretend the outside world didn't exist. But they didn't have that choice. They had families. Businesses. Responsibilities. And they couldn't take care of any of those if they were dead.

And while nobody knew where they were now, somebody might figure it out. So they needed to figure out who that somebody was first.

"We can't," he said. "We need to leave."

"Where are you taking me?" she asked as she sat up and the sheet slipped lower, revealing all her sexy curves.

He just wanted to take her over and over again. But if they made love, he wouldn't be able to do what he had to. He would want to stay forever in this place where they'd made love.

"Are you taking me to another safe house?" she asked.

He shook his head and reluctantly replied, "I'm taking you to prison."

Chapter Fourteen

I'm taking you to prison.

His words rattled her. After that horrific day she'd watched her father die, Stacy had never intended to return to River City Maximum Security Penitentiary. Yet here she was, walking through the high fence—with armed guards standing watch in high towers.

Her stomach knotted with nerves and grief. As much as she had loved seeing her father, she'd hated coming to the prison. But since it was the only way she could spend time with him, she'd overcome her fears and reluctance. But she wouldn't be able to see him today.

She wouldn't be able to see him ever again. Because of this place, she'd had to bury him. And she used to blame this man for his death. But this man was now her fiancé.

As they went through security, he watched her carefully—his blue eyes intense. He acted concerned and regretful. But if he were either of those things, he wouldn't have forced her to come back to this place. After they cleared security, a heavily armed guard escorted them to another part of the prison—away from the visiting areas and cells.

She had been there once—after her father died— to collect his last effects. The guard opened the door to the reception area for the warden's office. A young secretary glanced up from her desk. She flashed Logan a big smile and then spared Stacy a sympathetic glance. "You can have a seat. It'll be a few minutes before Warden Borgess can see you."

Logan nodded at the woman before steering Stacy toward chairs at the other end of the reception area as if he didn't want the secretary to overhear the conversation he anticipated them having.

"I don't understand why you think we had to come here," she said for the umpteenth time. But he had yet to answer her. So they actually hadn't had much of a conversation yet. "If it's to find out what my father's last words were, you're wasting your time."

"And keeping that secret is probably how you've endangered your life," he said.

"I've endangered *my* life?" she repeated, anger replacing her sadness at being back at the prison. "You're blaming *me* for the bombs and the shootings?"

He glanced toward the secretary, who was either fascinated with their argument or probably just with him. Then he lowered his voice, as if that might make Stacy do the same. "That isn't what I meant."

"It wouldn't be the first time you've blamed me," she said. "When you confronted me at my father's funeral, you thought I was the one shooting at you." And that same day they'd become engaged and then hours later they'd made love. Maybe grief over her father's death had addled her mind so that she'd acted more impulsively than she ever had in her life. But making love with him had actually been the most impulsive thing she'd ever done.

"I didn't think you were personally shooting at me," he said.

"You thought I put my brothers up to it."

"That was before I learned you really don't have that much control over them."

She felt as though she no longer had any control over any aspect of her life. Hopefully the ATF had cleared her building so that she could go back to the store and the workshop behind it. She needed to design something. She needed to control something—even if it were only metal and stones. But even if her building was reopened, it still wouldn't be safe—not until she and Logan caught whoever was trying to hurt them.

That was why she had put aside her fears and anguish and agreed to return to the place where her father had suffered and died. "I don't understand what you think we're going to find out here."

"Neither do I." Warden Borgess stood in the open doorway to his office. But he held out his hand to Logan and shook it heartily. Then he awkwardly patted Stacy's shoulder just as he had the day her father had died. That day he'd been full of guilt and regrets. "I still can't understand what happened to Mr. Kozminski. None of the other prisoners had *ever* showed any ill will toward him…" He shook his head.

Logan's brow furrowed. "So that attack on him was not provoked?"

Stacy gasped that he could still think so little of her father. But then he still believed that he had killed his father.

"Absolutely not," the warden said, as astonished by the comment as Stacy was. "Nobody had bothered Patek until that day."

"Is it possible to speak to the prisoner who attacked him?" Logan asked.

Fear clutched Stacy's heart, squeezing it tightly. She didn't know how Logan had confronted the man he believed had killed his father; she didn't want to ever see the monster who'd taken hers. She'd already had enough nightmares about him.

Borgess shook his head.

"If you asked, he might be willing to speak with us," Logan said.

The warden shook his head again. "No, it's not possible. The man died that very same day."

Stacy gasped again. "What?"

"I tried to let you know," the warden said, "but you didn't return the messages I left for you."

She hadn't wanted to hear from the warden again—or from anyone else associated with the prison that had taken away her dad.

He continued, "I figured you were busy planning services for your father."

She nodded. She had been busy planning the services. But Logan Payne had forced those plans to go awry. Instead of mourning her father, she'd gotten engaged.

"Who killed him?" Logan asked.

Borgess shrugged. "I don't know."

"You must have seen something on security cameras."

"The camera in that area had malfunctioned that day."

"So it was premeditated. Someone had messed with the camera before they attacked him. That someone must have had easy access to that area."

"All the prisoners do," the warden replied a bit defensively. Had he thought Logan was implying that a guard had killed the man?

Was that what Logan was implying?

"I'd like to see the visitor logs for that prisoner," he said.

Warden Borgess narrowed his eyes. "As I understand it, Mr. Payne, you're no longer with the

River City Police Department. Aren't you private security now?"

"Yes, that's why I'm here. Stacy's life is in danger and I'm trying to find out why someone set a bomb in her apartment on the day her father died."

The warden's eyes opened wide with alarm. "Are you all right, Miss Kozminski?"

She nodded. "Logan defused it."

The warden turned back to her bodyguard/soon-to-be husband. "You must be very good at your job, Mr. Payne."

"That's why I'm here," Logan repeated. "That's why I need to see who'd been visiting the prisoner who killed Mr. Kozminski."

"From your years with the River City Police Department, you must remember the law and the privacy rules that prevent me from giving you that information without a warrant," he replied almost regretfully.

"What about Stacy's father? Will we need a warrant to see his logs?"

"All you need is Ms. Kozminski's permission. She was his power of attorney and legal representative."

Both men turned to her, but Stacy hesitated. She wasn't certain what Logan hoped to gain by looking over visitor logs for either prisoner.

"If we're going to find out who's after us, we need to get as much information as we can," Logan said.

It was true. It was why they were there. She nodded her agreement. "Yes, I'd like to see the logs."

Borgess turned back toward his office. "I will personally pull those from my computer and print them out. It will only take a moment."

A moment for fifteen years of visits? Was that how few people had visited her father?

Regret and loss pulled heavily on Stacy, and she dropped back into the chair she'd been sitting in before the warden had stepped out of his office.

"Are you okay?" Logan asked, his deep voice vibrating with concern.

"Can I get you anything?" the secretary inquired.

Her father. That was all she wanted back. But he was gone forever.

Maybe that was why she had become engaged to Logan, why she'd left her family to be with him. So she wouldn't feel so alone. But she knew that he wasn't going to stay her fiancé, let alone ever become her husband. As soon as they were safe again, they would break up.

WARDEN BORGESS WAS only gone a few minutes. But it felt much longer, and with each second that ticked past, Stacy had grown more pale and shaky. If she hadn't already thought Logan was an uncaring jerk, she certainly would have after today.

He never should have brought her back here. Forcing her to do so had been heartless and insensitive. But the warden wouldn't have handed over the visitor logs, as he was now, without Stacy's permission.

"If there's anything else I can do for you, please let me know," the warden said, but he spoke to Stacy, his gaze warm with concern and maybe attraction. He was a young warden, and his ring finger was bare.

But then so was Stacy's and she was engaged now. He really should have gotten her a ring...

"We'd also like her father's personal effects," Logan added.

"I already gave those to Ms. Kozminski," Borgess said. "The day her father died."

The day the bomb had been set to blow up her apartment and anyone and anything inside it. The minute they'd stepped through the door, the timer had been tripped so that it had begun counting down the less than a minute they would have had to get out of the place. Was that why it had been set—to destroy whatever Patek Kozminski might have left behind?

He couldn't share his suspicions with Stacy in front of the warden, though. He didn't entirely trust the man. The prisoner who'd killed her father had turned up dead a bit too conveniently and easily for Logan's peace of mind. Because he didn't want to reveal any of his theories, he even waited until they'd exited the prison gates and climbed back inside the damaged black SUV before looking at the logs.

Stacy sat quietly in the passenger's seat as if the prison visit had physically drained her. But then she hadn't gotten much rest—because they had been too busy making love to sleep.

"What do you see?" she asked.

"A woman who loved her father very much," he replied honestly as he brushed a strand of hair back from her face and tucked it behind her ear.

She shivered, but it wasn't from cold. Maybe his touch had given her chills. She sighed and said, "I meant in the logs."

He'd perused them quickly but one name had kept jumping out at him. "I saw that in the log," he said. "In how many times you visited him."

She shrugged. "It wasn't enough."

"Once a week?"

She uttered another shaky sigh. "That was all that was allowed, but I wish it had been more."

"At least you came as often as you could," he said. "I still feel guilty for all those times I blew off watching a game or going to the restaurant with my old man so that I could hang out with my friends instead."

"You were a teenager," she excused him. "Teenagers think they and everyone around them are immortal."

Her visits hadn't been any less frequent when

she'd been younger. She'd always made time for her father. But then she'd already known there was no such thing as immortality or her dad wouldn't have been in prison for taking a life.

But had he taken it?

Maybe Stacy was getting to him, but he was beginning to have his doubts. He was beginning to wonder if she was right. That her father and his hadn't been alone that night that one of them had died and the other had been arrested for it.

"Nobody's immortal," he murmured as he started the SUV. "That's why we need to figure out who's after us. Because eventually we're not going to survive the bombs or the gunshots."

She shuddered.

"That's why I brought you here," he said as he drove out of the prison lot. "I wouldn't have put you through coming back here for any other reason."

"You weren't just torturing me?"

"I don't want to hurt you." That was why he'd tried to resist her last night; he hadn't wanted to take advantage of her vulnerability. But she'd wanted him. Last night. Today she would barely even look at him.

"Not anymore," she said of his statement.

"I never wanted to hurt you," he said. "That's not why I showed up at your father's parole hearings. I just wanted justice for my father." But now he wondered if in that quest for justice a horrible injustice had taken place.

"Then you should find out who really killed him," she suggested.

He nodded in agreement. "I intend to look into it more," he said. "I want to know the truth."

She grasped his arm. "Thank you. Thank you for listening to me."

It wasn't just her certainty that had given him doubts but also what he'd found in the visitor logs. Instead of taking the turn toward the city, he turned toward the rural outskirts. "That's why we're going to talk to someone else who was there that night."

"Your father's old partner? You're not going to learn the truth from him. For fifteen years, he's been blaming my father."

"Then why has he been visiting him nearly as often as you have?"

She sucked in a breath. Of shock.

Logan had felt the same way when he'd seen the name on the visitors logs. Shocked. And confused. He probably would have felt the same way over his mother's name appearing frequently in the logs—if she hadn't already admitted to visiting the man. But his mother's visits made more sense; she was the forgiving sort. Robert Cooper wasn't.

"I don't like the man," she admitted.

Neither did Logan. When he had been with the police department, he'd never lost a partner. And since he'd gone into private protection, he had never lost a client. He couldn't understand how Robert Cooper had lost his partner.

"But you're right," she continued, "that we need to talk to him. He must know more about that night than he admitted—like who else was there."

"But why would he have let that person get away with murder?" Robert Cooper might not have been a good cop, but he'd still been a cop. And to let a criminal get away with murder…

She shrugged. "I don't know. Nothing about that night ever made any sense to me."

"But you were fourteen then and convinced that your father was the greatest man in the world." At seventeen, he hadn't been much older but he'd believed the same thing about his father. "What if we find out it really was your father who killed mine?" Would she be able to handle her father's guilt?

Her face grew pale again and her eyes widened with horror. "It wasn't my dad. It couldn't have been…"

Chapter Fifteen

But what if it had been?

Would Stacy be able to deal with her father not being the man she had always believed him to be? She'd known he was a thief. He had never hidden that from his family.

But a killer?

She couldn't accept that.

"Are you okay?" Logan asked again.

She nodded. Even if it was true, she would be okay. But *they* would never be okay. She wouldn't be able to be with him again knowing that her father took his father from him. She would never be able to make up for what he'd lost, never be able to give him enough love to make up for the love he'd lost.

Love?

Did she love Logan Payne?

Panic clutched her heart. *Damn it. Damn him...*

She had fallen for her fake fiancé. But those feelings would never be reciprocated—probably not even if they learned that someone else had killed his father. If she hadn't forced herself on him, would he have made love to her?

She doubted it.

"How much farther?" she asked. They'd been driving for a while on what had seemed like a rather circuitous route. But then through the trees sunshine glimmered off water. They'd been traveling around lakes.

"Not much," he replied. But despite the curvy roads, Logan had had more attention on the rearview mirror than the windshield.

"Is someone following us again?" she asked. Panic pressed on her lungs, stealing her breath. He'd saved them last night because whoever had been following them hadn't just wanted to know where they were going, they'd wanted them dead.

He shrugged. "Maybe…"

So that meant yes.

"Did you lose them?" she asked.

He shrugged again. "Maybe…"

But when he stopped the SUV, he kept his hand on his holster when he stepped out of it. He leaned back inside. "You can stay here," he suggested.

For her protection from whoever had followed them or from whatever his father's older partner might say about that night?

"I want to hear this, too," she said. "I want to know why he visited my dad." She'd looked at the logs and couldn't believe that the man who'd arrested her father had visited him more than his own brother had.

And even more than his sons had.

But then part of that time, they had been busy serving their own sentences behind bars. Because of her...

And Aunt Marta had never visited her brother-in-law. Which was odd given that before she'd married Uncle Iwan, she had dated Stacy's dad. But then he'd fallen for her mother or at least for her beauty. There wasn't much more to her mom than her looks, which she constantly used to find a richer, more successful man. That was why Stacy's dad had started stealing—to provide for the woman. But it had never been enough.

Too bad the woman hadn't realized that nothing was more valuable than love. True love.

If only Stacy could find that for herself...with Logan. But he was barely aware of her now, his hand on his weapon and his gaze scanning the trees surrounding the little log cabin where his father's old partner must have retired. With rough-sawn logs and a wraparound porch, it was rustic but charming.

Birds chirped, and brush and branches rustled from the feet of scurrying squirrels and chipmunks. She'd been a city girl her whole life, but she could see the appeal of such a remote area. The peace...

But then shots rang out, shattering the peace.

"DAMN IT!" LOGAN shouted as he crouched behind the driver's door he'd left open.

"Duck down!" he yelled at Stacy. But she'd already lain across the front seat as much as the seat belt she still wore allowed her to move.

Had they been followed from the prison as he'd suspected? Or were the shots coming from the house? When he looked back at the cabin, he noticed a gun barrel protruding from an open window.

"It's me, Cooper!" he yelled. "Don't shoot!"

"You've gotta be kidding me!" the older man said as he hurried out the front door, the shotgun slung over his shoulder. "I thought you were those damn kids…"

"Kids?" Logan asked, wondering why the retired cop would have been shooting at kids, either.

Robert Cooper shoved a shaking hand through gray hair that was standing on end. "They've been breaking into the summer cottages around here."

"So you were going to shoot them?" Logan asked. Had the retired cop lost it? He was older than Logan's dad would have been; Robert had been the senior officer of their doomed partnership.

"I was shooting up in the air, so I wouldn't hit anyone. I just wanted to scare 'em," Robert said.

"Mission accomplished." Logan glanced at Stacy, who was still crouched below the dash. "It's okay," he assured her. But he wasn't certain of that—if the old man had lost it…

"I wouldn't have fired if I'd realized it was you," Cooper said. "But you've never been here before—not like your brothers have."

His brothers were more forgiving than he was; Stacy could vouch to that.

"They've come up to fish on the lake with me," Robert continued. "Have you come up to fish, Logan?"

He had, but for information instead of actual fish. He replied, "I'm not the sportsmen my brothers are." He walked around the car and opened the passenger's door for Stacy.

"You didn't come alone?" Robert asked.

Stacy stepped out, and the older man uttered a loud gasp. "Is that the Kozminski girl?"

"Yes," she answered for herself.

The older man chuckled gruffly, awkwardly. "I never thought I would see the two of you together. Since you were kids, you've been sniping at each other."

But they weren't sniping at each other anymore. "Someone else is sniping at us," Logan said. "With guns—"

"I wouldn't have shot if I'd known it was you," the older man said again.

"I'm not talking about today," Logan explained. "We've been getting shot at the past couple of days and someone even set a bomb in Stacy's apartment."

The retired cop turned to her. "But you're all right? It didn't go off?"

She shook her head. "Logan defused it."

"He was with you then, too?"

"We're together now," Logan said. "We're actually engaged." Whether the engagement was real or not didn't matter...because the feelings between them—the complicated, messy feelings—were real.

The older man gasped again and pushed his knuckles against his chest, as if the news had shocked him so much he was having chest pains.

Logan started toward him. "Are you all right?"

He nodded. "I—I just can't believe you two could ever overcome your differences."

Logan wasn't certain how that had happened, either—except that he had finally stopped blaming Stacy for supporting her father and had begun to admire her fierce loyalty. "I'm not sure we're all that different," he admitted. "We both love our families. Our fathers..."

She turned toward him, her gray eyes showing her surprise and appreciation.

But the retired cop expressed his surprise with a coarse curse before adding, "Her father killed yours. I didn't think that was something you'd ever get over, Logan."

"My father didn't pull the trigger," she said.

"He told you that?" Robert asked. "He told you that he didn't do it?"

She shook her head. "He would never talk to me about that night. But I know he didn't do it—that he couldn't take another man's life."

"What did he tell you?" Logan asked the former officer.

The older man glared in annoyance. "You know what he told me. You read the report. You were in court for my testimony. Your father caught him stealing and they struggled over the gun."

"I'm not talking about what he told you that night," Logan clarified. "I'm talking about what he told you all the times you visited him in prison."

The retired cop's already ruddy face flushed deep red. "What are you talking about?"

Stacy held up the visitor logs that the warden had printed out for her. "It's on here—all your visits to my father."

"Several over the years," Logan said. "Almost regular visits. If you knew everything you needed to about the night my father died, why did you keep going back to talk to his killer—unless you knew that he wasn't the killer."

His face flushed an even deeper shade of red until he was nearly purple. But his voice was gruff with disappointment when he replied, "You let her get to you, Logan."

"She's convinced that her father didn't pull the

trigger," Logan said, "that someone else was there that night."

"There was," Stacy insisted.

Logan stepped closer to the porch, careful to stay between the loaded shotgun and Stacy. The ex-cop might not have been as forgiving as Logan had found himself to be regarding the daughter of the man convicted of killing his father.

"Did you see someone else?" Logan asked Robert. "Is that why you kept going to see Kozminski? To find out who was with him that night?"

The older man sighed. "There could have been someone else…"

"Why didn't that get into your report?" Logan asked. "Or your testimony?"

"There *may* have been someone else," he said. "But there was *definitely* Kozminski. He was there robbing the place. I wasn't going to let him get away with murder because of reasonable doubt."

Logan had it now. Reasonable doubt. And Robert Cooper must have, too, because he'd kept visiting Kozminski.

"Who was it?" Stacy asked. "Who did you see?"

The older man shook his head. "Just a shadow—fleeing the building. I would have given chase, but I wanted to make sure my partner was all right. I'd already fallen too far behind him during pursuit, and he wasn't answering his radio call."

Logan shuddered as he realized why: because his father had been lying dead on the jewelry store floor with Patek Kozminski standing over him. That was the image he'd always had in his head—the image Robert Cooper had put there with his report and his testimony. And that was why Logan had stayed so angry at Stacy's father.

"So you just decided to pin a murder on my father that he didn't commit?" Stacy asked, her voice rising with anger.

"He never denied it," Robert pointed out. "He never proclaimed his innocence."

No. He hadn't. And there was only one reason for that. "He was protecting someone," Logan said. "You must have suspected that, too."

Robert nodded. "That is why I kept visiting him. I wanted him to tell me. But he never admitted anything to me." The retired cop turned toward Stacy. "Did he ever tell you anything?"

She shook her head. "I already told you that he refused to talk to me about that night."

"Even the last time you saw him?" Robert asked. "He didn't even tell you on his deathbed?"

"No," she said. "He still wouldn't talk about what happened."

"He didn't say anything about my father at all?" Logan asked. If Patek Kozminski really had killed a man and was about to die himself, wouldn't he want to make amends? Penance? Beg for forgiveness? But an innocent man had no reason to ask for forgiveness...

Could Stacy have been right all this time? Her father had been stuck in prison for a crime he hadn't committed. Logan had wondered before if he could forgive her for what her father had done. But could she forgive him for helping keep an innocent man in prison?

"He didn't talk about your father," she said.

And he was grateful that she'd at least revealed that much about the words over which she had been so secretive.

"So he didn't say anything about who else was there that night?" the ex-cop persisted.

"No."

"He died protecting whoever else had been there," Logan said. So it had to have been someone close to him. Someone he'd loved...

Stacy must have come to the same realization because the color left her face, leaving her skin translucent except for the dark circles beneath her smoky-gray eyes. Because if her father had loved that person enough to protect him, she probably loved that person, too.

"He didn't say anything. But did he leave you anything?" Robert asked. The cop had retired a few years ago, but apparently he had not forgotten how to interrogate a suspect.

But Stacy wasn't a suspect. There was no way

that she had been there that night. She would not have let her father go to prison for something she'd done.

"Was there anything in his personal effects?" Robert probed. "A letter? A journal?"

She shrugged. "I don't know. I haven't gone through his stuff."

"Did the bomb destroy his things?" Robert asked.

She shook her head. "No. I didn't bring his effects home with me."

She hadn't gone home from the prison. She'd gone straight to a friend. And she must have brought her father's stuff with her.

Her eyes widened again, as if she'd followed Logan's train of thought, too. If there was something in her father's stuff, some kind of confession or evidence, then whoever had that stuff was in danger. She grasped Logan's arm and murmured, "We need to leave."

"Where are his things?" Robert asked.

Logan covered Stacy's hand with his and squeezed. He didn't want her to say anything else in front of the old cop. "It's okay," he told the man. "We've got it from here."

The retired cop stepped forward so abruptly that he nearly stumbled down the porch stairs. "No. You can't cut me out of this investigation. I've been working this case for fifteen years."

"No, you haven't," Logan said.

Robert pointed toward the log printouts in Stacy's hand. "You saw my visits. You know I have been trying to get to the truth."

"No," Logan repeated. "A real cop would have included everything he'd seen in his report and his testimony."

"And then Patek Kozminski wouldn't have gone to prison."

Stacy gasped.

"No," Logan said. "He'd still been caught in the commission of a felony. A man had died during that felony. He would have gone to prison for those charges, but the real killer wouldn't have been free the past fifteen years."

"You think Kozminski would have given him up in some kind of plea deal?" Robert asked.

Logan shook his head. "No. But I would have been looking for the killer. And I wouldn't have stopped until he was brought to justice." And he wouldn't stop now.

He opened the passenger's door for Stacy. But she hadn't yet slid into the seat when the shots rang out. Logan reached for his weapon and turned toward the older man. But Robert Cooper wasn't firing. His shotgun was still slung over his shoulder.

The shots came from behind the already battered SUV—from the street. They had been followed from the prison. Logan pushed Stacy into the vehicle and drew his gun. But the window of the passenger's door shattered as the shots nearly struck him. He had no protection. No time to return fire.

No time left...

Chapter Sixteen

Stacy couldn't stop shaking. Those shots had been so close, but not to her. Like always, Logan had protected her. But he wouldn't have been able to protect himself. He'd had no time to take cover. No time to draw his weapon.

Fortunately, the old cop had fired his shotgun. Tires had squealed as whoever had followed them sped off. Tires squealed now as Logan rounded one of the curves around the lakes.

She braced one hand on the dashboard and clutched the armrest with her other hand. "You're not going to catch them." Not with all the hairpin turns and two-track roads running off the main street. "They could have gone anywhere."

"I knew we were followed from the prison," he said, berating himself.

The only people who'd been able to follow him so easily were her brothers and whoever had driven them off the road the night before. As Logan had pointed out, her father had been protecting someone the past fifteen years—someone he'd loved. His brother or his sons?

She shook her head. It couldn't be any of them. Her family wouldn't have let her father spend fifteen years in prison for something he hadn't done. It had to have been someone else—someone who'd killed once and would have willingly killed again if any of the shots had struck Logan or her or if either bomb had exploded...

Bomb? What if one had been set at her friend's house? Hopefully the bomber hadn't figured out where she'd been staying since her father's death. But what if she'd been followed...

She reached for Logan's arm again, grasping it tightly as she gave him the address. "You have to take me there."

"Why?"

"It's where I left my father's things—the things the warden gave me that Dad had had at the prison."

"The letter or journal?"

"I don't know what was in the box," she said. "I didn't look through it." There could have been evidence in it—a deathbed confession. But she cared less about that and more about her friend's safety.

"Whoever's trying to kill you doesn't know that," Logan said. "They think your father told you something or gave you something."

"Right now the important thing is making sure my friend is safe." She reached inside her purse for her cell phone. The screen was black, the battery completely dead. "Damn it."

"You left your charger at your friend's," he surmised.

It wasn't the only thing she'd carelessly left there. "I thought I'd be going back there after the funeral."

Logan fell silent, but he kept driving just as fast as he had earlier—as if he were pursuing someone. Or running from someone. He was ignoring her now, but he hadn't ignored her last night.

Heat flashed through her at the memories of their lovemaking. She had no regrets about making love with him. Her only regret was putting her friend in danger.

"Please hurry," she said.

But he shook off her grasp. Then he handed her his cell phone. "Mine's charged. Call your friend."

She punched in the number she'd memorized long ago. But nobody answered. "It went to voice mail."

What if there was a reason for that? What if there had been another bomb? Tears of fear and concern stung her eyes. "I will never forgive myself if something's happened…"

Amber Talsma was more like a sister than a friend. They would have been sisters—if she and Milek hadn't broken up instead of getting married.

Panic clutched her stomach as Logan turned onto

the suburban street. What if the house was gone? Obliterated?

But then there would have been a police barricade and reporters. And there was nothing like that. The house stood in the middle of the well-maintained green lawn. With its fieldstone and shake siding, it had an open floor plan and several big bedrooms. That was how Amber had convinced Stacy to stay with her—because she had so much room.

Stacy hoped that Amber wouldn't regret having her stay. She hoped that she hadn't endangered her and the other person who lived with Amber and her little dog. The minute Logan pulled the car into the driveway, Stacy threw open her car door and ran for the house.

The front door opened and a child greeted her, propelling his small body into her arms. There was no man in Amber's life; just a boy.

"Are you okay?" she asked him, love warming her heart as she pulled him close. "Is your mother okay?"

"She's in the shower," the four-year-old replied. "I'm 'kay, Aunt Stacy."

"No, you're not," his mother said as she crossed the foyer. "You're in trouble for opening that door, mister." Amber's smile froze and she reached for the towel she'd wrapped around herself as she stared behind Stacy.

She turned back toward a clearly shocked Logan. She probably should have corrected his misassumption earlier about her friend being male. And she probably should have warned him about her nephew. He looked nearly as shocked as if she'd opened the door to a bomb.

AFTER A THOROUGH search, they concluded there was no bomb. Logan had cleared the house of explosives before they'd left Amber Talsma and her son. And now, as they drove away, Stacy was clearing the box of belongings Warden Borgess had given her.

"Is there anything in there?" he asked, glancing over at her. But then he returned his attention to the rearview mirror and the road ahead of them.

She uttered a broken sigh. "Nothing about your father's death."

He glanced over again to the stack of photos and cards through which she was thumbing. "He saved them all?"

"Yes, all of them," she replied, her voice shaky with tears. "Every card and picture I ever gave him."

"Did you give him pictures of his grandchild?" Logan asked. "That boy is your nephew, right?" Not only had he called her "aunt" but he was a gray-eyed blond-haired miniature of her brothers while the child's mom had red hair and green eyes.

She hesitated as if considering lying to him. "He

might just call me that because his mother and I are such good friends."

Before he'd learned Amber was a woman, he had thought they were more than friends, and he'd been ridiculously jealous. Because of the boy, they actually were more than friends; they were family. "Is he Garek's or Milek's son?"

She sighed and held up a picture of a pudgy baby. She had given her father photos of the child. "Milek, but he doesn't know."

"That's one hell of a secret to keep."

"Amber has her reasons."

"What are yours?" he asked, appalled that she would keep such a secret. Maybe she wasn't as loyal to her family as he'd thought she was. "He's your brother. You should tell him. I would tell Parker if he had a kid."

She chuckled. "If Parker's reputation is to be believed, he probably does."

He nearly chuckled at the thought of his twin with a kid. "There's no way. He would never be that careless."

But then it suddenly occurred to him that *he* had been that careless. He hadn't protected her when they'd made love. And if they had made a child together, he wondered if she would tell him. Or would she keep that secret as she had kept so many other secrets?

"Milek was careless," she said, "with Amber's

heart. He broke it when he broke off their engagement. She didn't want to use her pregnancy to keep him. She didn't want to trap him into marriage."

He knew Stacy really didn't want to marry him at all. If she were pregnant, she was as unlikely to share that information as her friend. He would have to make certain that no matter what happened between them that they stayed in touch.

"They wouldn't have had to marry for Milek to be part of the boy's life," Logan said. "He could still spend time with him—still support him."

"Amber's a lawyer," she informed him. "The assistant district attorney, actually. She supports herself."

"Is she really going to get a warrant for the visitor logs of the prisoner who killed your father?" he asked.

Stacy nodded. "Definitely. She knows how important it is that we find out why my father was killed."

"Because someone had wanted him silenced." Someone had been afraid that he might finally reveal who'd really killed his father. And if that someone was willing to have one relative killed, they were definitely willing to kill another. He shouldn't have brought her with him.

He should have asked Parker or one of the other bodyguards of the Payne Protection Agency—besides Candace—to keep her safe. But Stacy had insisted on coming along. She had even refused to give him the address he'd needed unless he brought her along.

"We're here," she said as he pulled onto a city street.

This wasn't a residential area of River City. It was the warehouse district, and none of these warehouses had been converted to condos as far as he knew.

"They really live in one of these?" he asked.

She pointed toward one. It was brick instead of the cold-looking metal of the other buildings. But it still looked more industrial than residential.

He pulled the SUV to the curb and parked. But before he could slide out from behind the wheel, Stacy grasped his arm. "You can't tell Milek that he has a son," she said.

"It's not my secret to tell," he told her.

"It's not mine, either," she said.

"Do you think Milek is going to be okay with that when he learns the truth?" he asked. "And he will someday. He's going to be furious with you."

She sighed. "He's going to be furious with me anyway." She glanced toward the warehouse. "I'm not sure I can do this."

"Then let me," he offered. But he wasn't eager to face her brothers, either—at least not Milek. It wasn't his secret to keep or expose, but he wished to hell that he'd never found out.

Stacy followed him to the front door, though. Or at least he assumed the electric overhead door was the front. It rolled up when Stacy pushed a button. There was a foyer of corrugated metal and brick and off that interior foyer was another door that opened as they approached it.

Garek filled the doorway. "Why did you bring *him* here?"

"Why shouldn't she have brought me?" Logan wondered. "Afraid I might check serial numbers and find some stolen property?"

Garek uttered a particularly crude curse.

"Hey, I'm going to be your brother-in-law," Logan goaded him.

"She might have fallen in love with you, but I haven't," Garek said.

Stacy's face flushed with bright color, but instead of addressing her brother's comment, she ignored it to ask, "Is Milek here, too?"

Logan hoped he wasn't. But the other man appeared behind Garek.

"I'm here," he said. "What's going on? Did you set a date for this farce of a wedding?"

Logan would rather plan a honeymoon than a wedding. The thought of a honeymoon—of several nights of making love like they had—filled Logan with need. If only they had been able to go away—just the two of them...

But it would never be just the two of them.

There would always be their past and the secrets between them.

"We're still not safe," Stacy answered her brother.

"There have been more attempts on your life?" Garek asked with a glare at Logan. "I thought you would keep her safe!"

"Obviously he has or I wouldn't be here," Stacy defended him.

"But it has to end," Logan said with a pointed glare of his own at Garek. He still couldn't look at Milek. "It has to end now."

"You really think we would hurt our sister?" Milek asked, his voice gruff with disappointment and hurt.

How would he feel when he learned he had lost three or four years of his son's life? Logan hated secrets; he'd had to keep clients' secrets before but Stacy wasn't *paying* him to protect her. She wasn't his client.

She was his fiancée, though. And after last night that felt more real than fake. And fiancée probably trumped client. So he had to keep her secret, too.

But she grabbed his hand and squeezed it in warning—as if she suspected he was tempted to tell the truth.

"People will take desperate measures to protect themselves," he said. "So maybe you would hurt your sister to protect yourself."

"Protect myself?" Milek repeated. "Nobody's trying to kill *me*."

"Protect yourself from going back to jail," Logan clarified.

Garek stepped back. "Check all the serial numbers you want. We're not criminals."

Logan wasn't so sure about that but he begrudgingly gave them the benefit of the doubt. "Maybe not anymore…"

"You just can't let go of the past, can you?" Garek said. "I don't know how you ever fell for Stacy. Our dad was hers, too."

Panic clutched his heart as he realized that her brother was right. He had fallen for Stacy. But he wasn't sure how, especially when he knew that he couldn't trust her.

"I'm not so sure that your father was the one who killed my father," Logan conceded.

Milek chuckled. "She really has gotten to you."

More than she knew…

"I kept telling you that Dad wasn't alone that night," she said.

"And he listened to you?" Garek asked, his gaze returning to Logan. His eyes narrowed in consideration.

"Did you think no one ever would?"

"I'm not sure anyone should have," Garek said with an apologetic glance at his sister. "When it comes to our father, Stacy is still a little girl idolizing her daddy."

And instead of understanding that like her brothers did, Logan had resented her love for her father.

"That might be the case," he said, agreeing with Garek to a degree. "But my father's partner just admitted he saw someone else that night."

Garek's tall body tensed. "Who did he see?"

"Just a shadow," Stacy said, almost as if reassuring her oldest brother. "But it proves there was someone else there that night. Someone else who shot Officer Payne."

Milek wistfully sighed. "I wanted to believe you, Stacy. I wanted to believe that Dad was innocent, but he would never talk about that night."

And that was ultimately what had convinced Logan. A guilty man would have begged for forgiveness at the end, may have written a letter of apology to the family he'd deprived of a father. "He probably wouldn't talk about that night because he was protecting someone."

"Someone?" Garek repeated, one of his blond brows arching with the question.

"I suspect one of you," Logan said. "Who else would he have willingly gone to prison to protect?"

Milek chuckled. "We were kids. We wouldn't have gone to prison."

"You were teenagers," Logan said. "You may have been tried as adults. Garek was—"

"When we killed a man in defense of Stacy," Garek finished for him. He turned to his sister. "How could you let him turn you against us?"

She flinched as if he'd slapped her. "All I want is the truth."

"Dad didn't tell you on his deathbed?" Garek asked.

"Your father didn't tell her which one of you was with him that night—which one of you really pulled the trigger and killed my father," Logan assured him. "So you didn't have to try to hurt her."

"I would never hurt *her*," Garek said. "But I can't say the same about *you*."

"Garek!" Stacy yelled. But it was too late. Her oldest brother was already swinging.

Logan dodged the first punch. But Milek swung, too, and his first connected with Logan's jaw, knocking him back. Then, enraged, they both jumped on him. Two on one wasn't fair.

But Parker and Cooper had teamed up to fight Logan before, when they were kids, and he'd prevailed then. But his brothers hadn't actually been trying to kill him.

The Kozminski brothers wanted him dead. And this wasn't a fight that Logan was sure he could win.

Chapter Seventeen

Curses and grunts filled the air in which fists flew and blood spattered. Logan could have pulled his gun—could have fired at them to stop the assault. But apparently he didn't want to kill her brothers.

Stacy couldn't say the same of Garek and Milek. They piled on Logan, pounding. Panic and fear burning in her lungs, she screamed at them to stop. And then she pounded, too, hitting and kicking her brothers. She grabbed their hair and tugged, pulling them back. Pulling them off the man she loved.

"Stop it! Stop it!" she screamed, in such a panic that she hadn't realized they'd already stopped.

Garek rubbed his head. "Damn it, Stace, you pulled out a handful of hair."

"He's my fiancé," she declared. "I want to marry him." And that was the truth.

"That's the last thing *we* want," Garek said, and he fisted his hands and turned back to Logan.

Milek had already climbed back onto her wounded fiancé, his arms raised to swing again.

Logan wasn't fighting them off; he had to be hurt. Maybe badly.

"It's what Dad wanted!" she yelled. "Dad wanted me to marry Logan. Those were his last words to me."

"What?" Milek asked, but he stopped fighting midswing.

"Why?" Logan asked that question. "Why would your father want you to marry me?"

She'd wondered that, too. She hadn't understood what he'd been telling her.

"He admired you," she said, and she dropped onto her knees next to her fiancé. He was bruised and his lip was oozing blood. But he sat up easily as if nothing was broken.

"He said you were a man of conviction. A man of integrity and honesty. That you fought for those you loved," she continued. "He didn't think I would be able to find a better man than you to marry."

"Dad really said that?" Milek asked, doubtfully. "His last words were about Logan Payne?"

She nodded.

"Why didn't you tell us this before?" Garek asked.

"Because it was personal," she said. And she'd been embarrassed that her father had spent his last living moments matchmaking. Maybe that was why she loved Penny Payne so much; she reminded Stacy of her father. "And it had nothing to do with either of you."

Garek snorted. "That was the usual for Dad. He was all about his little princess."

She winced at her brother's resentment. She had never heard it before. Could Logan be right about her brothers actually wanting to hurt her?

"He loved you both, too."

Garek laughed. "Then why was he training us to be thieves? He brought us along with him on jobs."

Oh, God, Logan had been right. "You were with him that night? That was why he never said anything? Why he served the sentence—to protect one of you?"

Garek laughed again—bitterly. "You didn't know our father at all, Stacy. He started bringing me and Milek out on jobs when we were twelve so that if we got caught, we'd only go to juvie. If one of us had been with him that night, he wouldn't have taken the rap for us. One of us would have taken it for him."

Pain and disillusionment overwhelmed her and she gasped. Logan's arm slid around her shoulders, and he pulled her tight to his side as if to protect her. He could save her from physical harm, as he had already so many times. But he couldn't protect her from emotional harm.

"I knew you were willing to hurt her," Logan said. "And you found the most painful way to do that."

Despite his swelling eyes, Milek glared at his

brother. "That was harsh," he admonished him. "She didn't need to know any of that."

"But was it true?" she asked.

"It wasn't so much that he forced us to steal," Milek said. "It's just what was expected of us as Kozminskis. Our traditional profession is jewelry thief—like Payne's is law enforcement."

"And because of that," Garek said, "a Payne and a Kozminski should never marry. Dad was wrong about that, too."

She had asked them before, but since they were actually being honest now—brutally honest—with her, she asked again, "Is that why you've been trying to kill him?"

Garek cursed. "We haven't been trying to kill him."

Logan grunted in protest.

"Beating the crap out of you is different than shooting at you," Garek pointed out. "Besides, we don't even own a gun."

"Neither did Dad," Milek said. "The only Kozminski who ever owned one is Uncle Iwan."

"Iwan?" Logan asked.

"He wouldn't try to kill you," Stacy said. But her uncle had always been an enigma to her. Unlike her charming father, Uncle Iwan had always been quiet and withdrawn—as if fearful to speak up in front of his overbearing wife.

Garek moved and grunted. "I wouldn't be too sure about that."

"But why?" Stacy asked. "To avenge our father?"

But according to the logs, he hadn't even visited his brother that often. How close had they really been?

Milek shrugged. "That's what I thought. That it must have been him shooting at Logan since we knew it wasn't us." But he spared his brother a glance as if he wondered.

Hadn't Garek and Milek been together every time the shootings had happened?

"Maybe it wasn't Logan he was shooting at or trying to blow up," Garek said.

Stacy gasped. She and Uncle Iwan had never been close but… "Why would he want to hurt me?"

Garek mused, "Aunt Marta is really damn concerned about what our father told you on his deathbed. That's because she doesn't want to lose her meal ticket. She doesn't want Uncle Iwan going to jail."

Logan tensed. "You think your uncle was there that night? You think he's the one who killed my father?"

"But why would Dad take the rap for him?" Milek asked.

Garek pointed at her. "So she would have a legal guardian. He'd been caught stealing. He was going to jail no matter what, and he didn't want our mother getting custody. He wanted Uncle Iwan to take her. To protect her."

Tears stung her eyes. "Do you hate me?" she asked her brother.

Garek leaned forward and cupped her face in his palm. "I love you. You're my little princess, too, Stace. I would do anything to protect you. That was why I never told you about Dad. I wanted to leave you that fantasy you had of him being such a good man."

"But he wasn't?" Logan asked the question.

"He was a thief," Garek said, and a trace of self-loathing replaced his earlier bitterness.

"But he wasn't a killer," Milek said. "Stacy has been right about that. He taught us how to bypass security systems and break into safes and vaults. He taught us how to use tools, not guns. He never wanted us to carry a weapon. He wouldn't have had the gun that night."

"But your uncle has a gun?" Logan asked. "You've seen it?"

Stacy nodded. "He showed it to me when I first came to live with him and Aunt Marta."

Logan's brows rose in surprise. "He showed a teenage girl a gun? To scare you?"

"To make me feel safe," she said. "I had nightmares—because of what happened…"

"With our stepfather," Milek said, as if wondering if she'd told Logan.

"The pervert," he said—the bitterness all his now.

Garek nodded heartily in agreement. "He sure was."

Logan's arm tightened around her.

Garek added, "You're safe now, Stace."

But Logan shook his head. "She won't be safe until we figure out who's been trying to kill her."

"And you," Milek added, as if he cared.

How could men pound on each other one minute and bond the next? Even though she'd been raised with them, she would never understand them.

"I'm more concerned about Stacy," Logan said, but even as he said it, he was easing away from her. "Can you guys keep her safe?" He stood up as if he was leaving.

She stood up, too—so quickly that she was dizzy for a moment. He grabbed her shoulders and steadied her. "Where are you going?" she asked. But she knew.

"I have to do this…"

"I know," she said. "But I'll go with you."

"We can all go," Milek offered.

Logan shook his head. "I have to do this alone."

"That makes no sense," Stacy said. "You don't have to—"

"It was his father who died," Garek said. "So he has to do this alone."

For vengeance? Was he going to kill her uncle?

LOGAN WAS MAD enough to kill. But he was madder at himself than anyone else. Why hadn't he more thoroughly investigated his father's death? Sure, he'd been a kid when it had happened fifteen years ago. But since then he'd gotten a degree in criminal justice and then had become a cop before his quick promotion to detective.

He should have looked into it more—should have gone over the reports and the testimony with more scrutiny. He should have listened to Stacy.

Sure, her brothers were right that she had idolized—or rather idealized—her father. But even they had had to admit that he wasn't a killer. He'd never even carried a weapon on him. So where had that gun come from? The gun with which Logan's father had been killed?

Had it been one of Iwan Kozminski's? If so, he must have replaced it with the gun that he'd showed Stacy. To reassure her and stop the nightmares? Or to scare her?

Her uncle wasn't the loving male figure her father had been. Even from behind bars, her father had tried to protect her—so much so that he'd been willing to take the rap for another man's murder. Sure, he hadn't been the completely innocent man Stacy had believed him to be, but neither had he been the monster Logan had considered him all these years.

Did Stacy consider *him* a monster? And not just for keeping her father in prison but for what she was afraid he might do to her uncle? He wouldn't kill anyone except in self-defense. He could have pulled his gun on her brothers and saved himself the split lip and bruised ribs that throbbed with pain. But Stacy loved her brothers so much that she would never forgive him taking one of their lives.

And she'd saved him. She'd fought at Logan's side instead of against him. She'd acted like his partner, like his wife. Maybe he should have let her come along today. But he trusted her aunt and uncle even less than he trusted her brothers.

As they'd been the night before, the gates to the Kozminskis' estate stood open, as if they were expecting him again.

Had Garek or Milek called ahead to warn their uncle?

He reached for his holster to make sure his gun was easily accessible. Then he parked the SUV and approached the three-story brick mansion.

Suddenly the front door opened and Iwan stepped outside with narrowed eyes. "What are you doing here?" he asked nervously.

"Were you expecting someone else?" A long black car pulled through the open gates. And Logan noticed the suitcase Iwan Kozminski pulled behind him. "You're leaving town?"

"I—I need to make a business trip," he replied.

"What exactly is your business, Mr. Kozminski? I've never been told what you do for a living." He assessed the impressive house. "But you must do it very well." He hadn't been caught like his brother had been. Or maybe he'd just run faster...

"Who's here?" a female voice asked. Marta Kozminski stepped out of the foyer, a drink in her hand. "Oh, *you*..." She swirled the ice cubes and stared down into the liquid as if unable to meet his gaze.

He had no warrant. No legal way to keep Iwan from leaving the country, which was what he was certain he was doing, so Logan asked, "Can you take a later flight? I'd really like to talk to you."

"I can't imagine what we have to talk about," Iwan replied. "We barely know each other."

"And yet we're going to be family," Logan reminded him.

"I don't understand why his niece would ever marry you," Marta said. "That girl has always been strange, though."

Because she'd been self-sufficient? Because she cared more about people than money? He bit his tongue to keep from uttering those questions. But he couldn't stay silent. "She's an amazing woman."

Iwan sighed and waved off the car. "I'll take a later flight."

Marta shook her head. "You don't have to talk

to him. He's not a police officer anymore. He's not really even family."

"I will be," he promised her.

She flounced back into the house. Probably to pour another drink. Iwan stepped back to escort Logan inside. He wondered if he should have brought backup. Not Stacy or her brothers but maybe his brother. His family deserved the truth about their father's death, too.

But that was why he hadn't called any of them. He didn't want to say anything until he knew the entire story. He didn't want to bring up all that pain and all those bad memories until he'd found the person who was really responsible for their father's death.

"What do you want to discuss with me?" Iwan asked as he led the way through a marble-floored foyer to a darkly paneled den. "Stacy's brothers?"

"Those hooligans," Marta snarkily remarked from where she stood at the bar, pouring herself another drink just as he suspected. She glanced up and pointed toward his face. "Did they do that to you?"

"Yes," he answered.

"Animals…"

He wasn't so sure about that anymore. Maybe their pounding on him had addled his brain, but he had actually begun to trust them—or he never would have left Stacy in their protection. But what if that had been a mistake? An even bigger one than coming here without backup?

"They love their sister, though," he said. He had to convince himself of that or he would rush back to make sure she was all right with them, that they hadn't hurt her.

"Maybe too much," Marta said. "Since they went to prison for her."

They had been willing to do time to keep her safe; they wouldn't have let their father do time for their crime. Robert Cooper had to have seen someone else that night.

"Their father went to prison for her, too," Logan said.

"He went to prison for killing your father," Marta heartlessly reiterated. "How could you have forgotten that?" Obviously she didn't want him forgetting.

"That's the crime he was convicted of," Logan agreed. "But it wasn't the one he committed."

Iwan studied him. "I didn't believe my brother could ever take a life, especially the life of a policeman. But I thought *you* were convinced of his guilt."

"He was guilty," Marta anxiously insisted. "Did he say something else to his daughter? Did he make some crazy claims on his deathbed?"

That Logan was the man for her—that had been a crazy claim. How had Patek Kozminski ever thought that a relationship between them would work?

"The arresting officer is actually the one who made the claim—that there was someone else there that night," Logan said. "He saw that someone…"

Iwan shrugged. "Then why didn't he testify to that? Why didn't it even get into his report?"

"He wanted to make sure that your brother was convicted. But he never stopped looking for the man he saw that night, the one that I believe actually pulled the trigger." He focused on the older man, studying his face for any sign of guilt. But the guy was so controlled, probably from all those years of being a jewelry thief. "Was it you?"

"Drop it!" Marta screamed. "Just drop it!"

"I can't," Logan said. "I need to know the truth. I need to know who really killed my father." But from the corner of his eye, he caught the glint of metal.

Marta brandished a gun. "Drop it!" she yelled again.

But instead of giving up his weapon, Logan pulled it and pressed it to her husband's chest. "I don't care if she shoots me, I want the truth before I go. I need to know. Was it you that night?"

"I told the officer that Iwan was with me that night," she said, hysteria making her voice shrill. "He was with me!"

"And you wouldn't lie for your husband?" he scoffed. "I don't believe you." He turned back to Iwan, but even with the gun pressed against his chest, the man betrayed no emotion—not guilt or even fear. "You and your brother were thieves together."

"He was teaching his sons, too," Marta said.

"But it wasn't them."

"It wasn't me," Iwan said, and finally he nervously glanced down at the gun pressed to his chest. "I wasn't with him that night."

Marta sucked in a breath as if she was surprised by the news.

"He wasn't with you, either," Logan surmised and he eased back with the gun. The safety was on; he wouldn't have actually pulled the trigger. He wasn't so sure about Marta Kozminski. "So *where* were you?"

The older man sighed. "You don't need to know that—you just need to know that I wasn't with my brother."

"Neither were his sons. So who could it have been? Was there someone else he worked with?"

"A cop," Iwan replied. "He had a cop in his pocket. That was how he'd gotten away with so many heists."

"Which cop?"

"I thought it was your father," Iwan said. "I thought that's what happened that night—that they had a disagreement over the percentage each would keep, and your father wound up dead."

Logan shook his head. "That's not possible. My father was not a dirty cop."

Iwan shrugged. "I don't know. I could have sworn it was him."

Was it possible that Logan hadn't really known his father? That like Stacy had hers, he had idealized his dad, too?

"I want to know," Marta said, and now she swung the gun toward her husband. "I want to know where you were that night. All these years I thought you were with him. I thought you pulled the trigger, too. I know Patek wouldn't have had the nerve."

"It wasn't me," Iwan insisted. "I wasn't there."

"Then where were you?" she screamed. She was drunk and now she was hysterical.

The situation had quickly gotten out of hand. Logan turned toward her and estimated if he could reach for the gun before she could fire it.

"Where were you?" she screamed again. And then her gaze grew wilder. "You were with her? That whore you've been seeing? The one you were probably going to meet today?"

Before Logan could grab the gun, she pulled the trigger. The bodyguard in him reacted, and he put himself in front of the bullet.

Chapter Eighteen

The shot reverberated outside Uncle Iwan and Aunt Marta's house. And a scream tore from Stacy's throat. She ran toward the house, but Garek caught her arms, trying to hold her back. She wriggled free of his grasp and ran inside. Her feet pounded across the marble floor of the foyer. "Logan!"

Hysterical cries emanated from the back of the house, from the area of the den. Stacy ran. But her brothers had caught up with her and beat her to the doorway.

"Damn it, Aunt Marta!" Garek exclaimed. "You killed him!"

Pain clutched Stacy's heart, and tears burned her eyes. "No! No!"

She pushed past Milek so she could see. Two men lay on the floor in a pool of blood. Logan and her uncle.

Aunt Marta stood over them, her hand shaking with the gun that Garek quickly wrestled from her grasp. "Give me the gun, Marta!"

Stacy dropped to her knees beside her fiancé. "Logan! Logan!"

His eyes—those brilliant blue eyes—opened and focused on her face. And relief flooded her.

"She has a gun," he warned her, clasping her close as if to protect her. Blood from his shirt stuck to hers, staining it.

"Garek got it away from her," she reassured him.

And in the distance sirens whined. Police were on the way.

"Where are you hurt?" she asked, her fear and panic rushing back over her. "Where did you get shot?"

He touched his side. "I tried to stop her. Tried to step in front of it…"

He hadn't been her intended target?

"How's Iwan?" Logan asked, and with only a slight grimace, he rolled toward the older man. "Did he get hit?"

Uncle Iwan's eyes were closed and blood oozed from a wound in his chest. Logan touched his neck. "He has a pulse. Call an ambulance."

"Cheating swine," Marta cursed her husband. "He better not make it."

"If he doesn't, you'll spend the rest of your life in prison," Logan warned her. He might have been wounded, but not so badly that he was weak from the injury.

And a short while later, officers led her off in

handcuffs while paramedics loaded Uncle Iwan into the back of an ambulance. Logan refused to ride in one, so Milek drove him and Stacy in his car while Garek followed in the battered SUV.

Parker and Nikki and Mrs. Payne met them at the hospital. "I'm okay," he told his family as they rallied around him. "It was a through and through. How's Iwan?"

"They took him to surgery," Garek replied. "His condition is serious, but not critical."

Parker slammed his fist into Garek's jaw. "You did this. You shot my brother."

Milek grabbed Parker and shoved him back. "Get off my brother!"

"Stop," Logan yelled, then grimaced and grabbed his side. "They didn't do this. Marta was trying to shoot her husband and I stepped in front."

"You've been shot again," Mrs. Payne exclaimed, her eyes glistening with tears. Her slight body began to tremble. Stacy reached out to her, putting her arm around the older woman.

"It's a through and through," he repeated. "I'm fine." And a short while later, a doctor agreed with him when he pronounced it okay for a bandaged Logan to leave the hospital.

"Uncle Iwan's still in surgery," Garek told her. "And Aunt Marta's getting booked."

Stacy was more concerned with her new family than her old family. She had stayed with Mrs.

Payne and Nikki while Logan had been getting examined and x-rayed. Parker had paced and talked on his cell phone. He pocketed the phone now and told his twin, "They're going to run ballistics on that gun and find out if Marta was the one shooting at you and Stacy."

Logan nodded. "That's good. I'm not sure she would have known how to make those bombs, though..." His voice trailed off on a slur. He was completely exhausted.

Because of her family...because of her...

"Let me take you home," she said.

He shook his head.

And her pride stung and pain squeezed her heart. He was rejecting her.

"Not home. To *our* place," he said. "Where we went last night..."

Where they had made love. She wasn't sure how to get there since she'd slept during the ride. But she didn't admit that until they had said goodbye to everyone and were alone in the car.

As exhausted as he was, he insisted on driving to make sure that they weren't followed. But he winced and grimaced every time he turned the steering wheel.

"You shouldn't be driving."

"I'm fine," he insisted. And he proved it by making it safely to the town house. But as soon as they were in the elevator, he leaned heavily against one of the walls. So Stacy slid beneath his arm and wrapped her arm around his uninjured side to keep him on his feet.

"You're not fine," she said.

"If we get married, you're going to have to promise to stick by me in sickness and health," he threatened.

"If we get married…" It wasn't likely to ever happen. Their engagement hadn't stopped the attempts on their lives. How would a wedding?

"I'll also have it put in the vows that you always have to be honest with me," he added.

Obviously it was still bothering him that she was keeping a secret—a big, almost four-year-old secret—from her brother. "I have been honest with you," she said.

"Always?"

"I haven't lied to you," she said.

"But there's more to being honest than just telling the truth," he stubbornly persisted. "There's being open and forthcoming. Being honest means no secrets."

The elevator stopped on the top floor and saved her from replying. Because if she agreed, she would have to tell him how she felt about him—that she loved him.

But maybe she didn't have to tell him to be honest about her feelings. Maybe she could just show him. So she unbuttoned his bloody shirt and pushed it from his shoulders. Then she unsnapped his jean and lowered his zipper and helped him take off his pants. Then she gently pushed him back onto the bed and joined him.

He groaned.

"Are you in pain?" she asked, concern stilling the fingers she'd run over his chest. He had a blood-stained bandage on his shoulder and another on his side. And his skin was bruised and swollen in places. But other parts of him were swelling, too, in reaction to her touch.

"You can ease my pain," he said.

She kissed his chest, gently touching her lips to each bruise. Then she moved to each nipple and then to each ripple of muscle as she moved over his washboard abs to his hips.

He groaned as her lips closed over him, and she drew him into her mouth. But he pulled her up before she could give him pleasure.

His hands shook as he removed her clothes. He cupped her breasts and teased her nipples with his thumbs and then with his lips. And his hand moved lower, between her thighs.

She squirmed as pleasure shuddered through her. He'd barely had to touch her to make her feel gratification. He lifted her thigh so that she straddled him, and he thrust inside her.

The pressure built again, winding tightly inside her. With his fingers skimming along her jaw, he tilted her head down and kissed her. His tongue moved between her lips, teasing and tasting her.

Her heart pounded heavily with excitement and desire. She had never wanted anyone as much as she wanted her fiancé. And as she climaxed again, she cried out with pleasure and nearly declared her love.

But then he was clutching her hips and thrusting deep as he joined her in release. With slightly shaking arms, he held her close—as if he never intended to let her go.

"I'm too heavy," she sleepily protested. "I don't want to hurt you." Blood was already seeping through the bandage on his side.

"Then stay where you are," he groggily replied. "Stay with me…"

Exhaustion finally claimed him, and he fell asleep. As he breathed evenly and deeply, his chest moved against her breasts. And she wanted him again. Still. Always…

She must have fallen asleep, though, because she didn't awaken until an alarm…or a phone…jingled. Her phone had died. So it must have been Logan's. She dragged herself from his arms and fumbled around in the dark, looking for his jeans that she'd discarded on the floor.

The phone rang again, the screen illuminating the pocket, so she finally found it. Because she recognized the number on the screen, she answered it.

"Stacy?" Amber asked.

"Yes."

"Are you all right?" her friend asked. "I heard about your aunt and uncle."

"Is he okay?" She should have called her brothers and followed up. But she'd been more concerned about her fiancé.

"He made it through surgery," Amber said, "and his prognosis is good. But I'm not actually calling about that. I got the warrant."

Stacy's breath caught with momentary fear. She'd wanted the warrant, but she didn't want to have to go back to the prison. "Okay, I'll see when Logan can drive back out to the penitentiary."

"He's not with the River City P.D.," Amber said. "He can't serve it, so I did it myself. I got the visitor log. I also looked at your father's. And there was one name in common."

Stacy's stomach knotted. But she had to know. "Who was it?"

"I need to report this to a detective with the P.D., too," Amber said. "But honestly, I'm not sure who to trust. This is bad, Stacy."

"Who?"

When she heard the name, she gasped. But it shouldn't have been that much of a shock; it should have been obvious to her. Her father had spent fifteen years in prison for this man's crime, but that sentence hadn't been bad enough, he'd ordered her father's death, too.

She clicked off the phone and sat on the side of the bed. The numbness of her father's loss began to wear off, leaving only crippling pain. It hurt. It hurt so much to have lost him. Maybe he wasn't the perfect daddy the little girl in her remembered. But he hadn't deserved to die like he had. He hadn't deserved fifteen years locked up like an animal.

The bed shifted as Logan rolled over and stretched. Then he groaned, probably in pain from his injuries.

"Are you all right?" she asked, and her voice cracked with her grief.

"I'm fine," he said. "But you're not. Who was on the phone?"

She didn't want to tell him because she knew he'd want to go off alone again. But he'd asked her to always be honest with him, to keep no secrets from him. "Amber."

"She got the warrant," he said.

She nodded.

"She gave you a name. You know who it is," he said. "You know who killed my father."

"And mine," she said. "There was only one person who visited both my father—frequently—and his killer."

"Cooper," he uttered the name like a curse. He was already climbing out of bed, already reaching for his clothes. She grabbed his arm, trying to stop him. Or at least slow him down.

"I don't want you to go alone, though."

"You're not going with me," he said. "I promised to keep you safe. I want you to stay here."

She wanted to believe he was so concerned about her safety because he loved her, too. But it was just who he was—a bodyguard.

"Call the police," she urged him. "I don't want you to put your life at risk again." He had already had many lucky escapes; his luck was bound to have run out by now.

His luck had run out. Robert Cooper realized it the moment that Logan Payne drove back into his driveway. The shotgun was loaded and sitting next to his chair. But he didn't reach for it. Yet.

He'd do what he had to do, though. He waited for the knock at the door, but Logan just walked right in, his gun drawn. Maybe he should let the boy have this—justice. It was long overdue.

Logan stared down the slightly unsteady barrel at the man he'd resented for the past fifteen years. He'd resented that his father's partner hadn't protected him that night. Now he knew that he should have hated the man because he hadn't just not protected him—he had killed him.

"Why?" he asked.

"You know why," the retired cop replied. He

looked older than his sixty-some years now. His sparse gray hair stood up, disheveled, and gray stubble clung to his sagging jowls.

Disgust overwhelmed Logan and he bitterly surmised, "Money."

"I had a deal with Kozminski," Robert said. "He cut me in for looking the other way."

"And my father?" Had he been a dirty cop like Iwan had implied?

Robert Cooper sighed. "He wouldn't look the other way. When he caught us that night, he was going to arrest us both, so I pulled my drop gun and killed him."

"And Kozminski went along with it?" Logan asked. "I don't understand why he wouldn't have told the truth."

"Because he loved his kids."

He tightened his grip on his gun. "You threatened them?" They'd just been kids then—younger even than he'd been.

"Yes," Robert replied. "And I would have followed through on the threat. I would have killed them. And he knew it. That's why he kept quiet all these years."

"Then why did you hire the other inmate to kill him?"

Robert shifted forward in his chair, but only to point a finger at Logan—not a gun. "That was your fault."

"Mine?"

He nodded. "You kept getting his parole denied. And he wanted out. He was going to talk."

A pang of regret struck Logan's heart. If only he had let Kozminski's parole get granted, Stacy's father might still be alive. Might've been able to walk her down the aisle...

To him?

She would never marry him. She would never forgive him for getting her father killed. She had been right about that.

Logan was the one who'd been wrong. About everything...

"Is that when you started shooting at me?" Logan asked.

The older man shook his head. "I never shot at you."

"You did the day I drove up here," Logan reminded him.

"I thought you were coming to arrest me," he said. "That you'd figured it out already."

"There were other shots fired that day," he said. "You must be working with someone else."

Cooper shook his head. "I haven't worked with anyone since Kozminski."

"There was the prisoner you had kill him..."

The older man shrugged. "Some people have owed me favors."

Logan's stomach churned with self-disgust that

it had taken him so long to figure out what should have been so obvious. "So if it hasn't been you shooting at me, it must have been someone who owed you a favor—because I've been shot at a lot over the past few days," he said. "Once at a safe house and then again at the church the day my brother Cooper got married."

"That wasn't me or anyone working for me," Robert insisted. "I made a promise to your father."

"After you shot him?"

The older man nodded. "I respected your father. He was a good man. I promised him that I would never hurt his wife or kids."

"But you promised Kozminski the exact opposite."

"They're Kozminskis," he said, as if that justified his actions. "They're all criminals."

"Stacy isn't. She's my fiancée."

"She wasn't when I set the bomb in her place or when I shot at her at the cemetery. I was sure the old man would have told her the truth, that he wouldn't have wanted to die with his baby girl believing he was a killer."

She was more loyal than that. "She never believed it," Logan said. And he should have trusted her instincts sooner.

"She's a stubborn woman," Robert remarked. "She's going to be a challenge as a wife."

Getting her to be his wife would be the challenge.

But Logan had a bigger challenge at the moment—getting the loaded shotgun out of Robert Cooper's reach before he used it. But before he could move toward it, the old man grabbed it, aimed and fired.

Chapter Nineteen

Stacy's scream echoed the gunshot.

But this time Milek and Garek held her back from rushing toward the house—toward Robert Cooper's cabin. Garek reminded her, "He warned us that Cooper could have rigged his place with a bomb."

That was why they'd picked up Cujo from the kennel and brought him along. Parker had snuck him in the back door while Logan had calmly walked in the front to confront his father's killer.

Had he become the man's most recent victim?

Her heart pounded frantically. And she trembled. She couldn't lose Logan. He wasn't just her fake fiancé. He was the love of her life. When he finally stepped out onto the porch, she wanted to run to him, wanted to throw her arms around him and never let go.

But she couldn't move. Her legs kept shaking. She had to wait until he walked down to her and her brothers. Her breath caught as she noticed that blood spattered his handsome face. "Are you—" she stammered. "Are you all right?"

He ran his hand over his face and smeared the blood. "Yeah, it's all over now. He killed himself."

"Is it all over now?" Parker asked as he brought Cujo around from the back of the house.

"Did that damn dog find another bomb?" Garek asked.

Parker shook his head. "No, but the old cop denied ever trying to kill Logan."

Logan snorted. "And you believe him?"

"He admitted to everything else," Parker said. "Why lie about that?"

"Because he's the person who killed our father and framed another man for it," Logan replied.

"Why didn't our dad tell the truth?" Garek asked.

Logan glanced at Stacy. "Because he was threatened."

"What more could Cooper do to him?" Milek wondered.

"Take away his family," Logan said. "He threatened to kill all of you if your father didn't keep his secret."

The color fled from Garek's face, leaving him pale and shaky. "He really did love us."

She squeezed his arm. "All of us," she said. "He loved all of us."

"Why'd the crazy cop kill him now?" Milek asked.

Logan grimaced. And she worried that he'd re-injured himself. But then he said, "It was my fault. If I hadn't fought his parole…"

He blamed himself…like she had been blaming him for years. But she couldn't do that anymore. Her brothers, however, didn't love Logan like she did.

"You got him killed," Garek accused him. "It's all your fault!"

Parker stepped forward with a snarling Cujo. "Take that back. Logan has risked his life over and over to save Stacy's. He loves her."

If only that were true…

But apparently Logan didn't share that infamous psychic connection with his twin.

"It's okay," Logan said with a reassuring pat on Cujo's head. "I understand…"

"I think you were right," Parker said. "I think these guys are behind the attempts on your life."

Was that true? Had Robert Cooper really not shot at Logan? Had that been one of her brothers?

"It could have been Aunt Marta," she offered.

Parker nodded. "Could have been. The forensics haven't come back on her gun yet."

But Marta really had no reason to avenge her brother-in-law's death. She hadn't cared about him; she'd only cared about keeping her husband and her lifestyle. It could have been her brothers. "Or it could have been that Candace woman," Stacy suggested—a bit desperately. She couldn't lose another member of her family. "She's been desperate to protect you…"

"She was with me the first time I was shot at," Logan remarked. "It wasn't her."

And it probably wasn't. She would have tried to kill Stacy but not the man she loved.

"So what you're saying is that there's someone out there still—someone who wants to kill you?" Stacy asked as she realized that she was bound to lose Logan.

SOMEONE WANTED HIM DEAD.

His future brothers-in-law or someone else?

It wasn't Candace. She stood before him now, her letter of resignation on his desk between them. He had no idea when she'd left it there. This was his first time back in the office—the afternoon after his father's killer had killed himself.

"Is this what you want?" he asked.

"I can't have what I want." Her face flushed as she must have realized how her remark sounded. "I'm sorry."

She shook her head. "No. I should have known that you only saw me as an employee."

"And a friend," he corrected her.

"You never looked at me the way you look at Stacy, the way you looked at her even before your engagement," she said with a wistful sigh. "You love her."

He did love her. "Is that why you're giving me this?" He pointed at the letter.

She shook her head. "I figured she told you and that neither of you would want me working for you anymore."

"I don't want to lose one of the best damn guards I've ever had." He ripped up the resignation. "Will you stay on?"

She nodded. "I've heard you still need protection yourself. Your father's old partner claims he wasn't the one taking the shots at you." Parker must have filled her in.

"O'Doyle from the ATF doesn't think he set the second bomb, either."

"The one at Parker's?"

He nodded.

"Do you think her brothers are behind it?" she asked.

He hoped not. But he'd called them to his office, too. They passed Candace on her way out. Garek whistled at her, which elicited a glare.

"You must have a death wish," Logan remarked. "She could easily kill you."

"It might be fun to go out that way," he murmured appreciatively.

Milek grabbed his brother's arm and tugged him fully into Logan's office. "We're not here for fun."

"No, we're here for an interrogation," Garek surmised. "Let me spare you the inquisition. It's not us. We're not trying to kill you."

"Someone is," Logan said.

"You proved it wasn't the dirty cop?"

He nodded.

"Then you know what you have to do," Garek said.

"Of course," Logan replied. "I have to find out whoever's after me."

"You have to let Stacy go," Garek corrected him. "As long as you're still in danger, so is she."

Milek sighed and ruefully agreed. "He's right. Someone could accidentally shoot her while they're trying to hit you."

Logan flinched as he realized that they made sense. He was putting her in danger.

"You promised to keep her safe," Garek reminded him.

"And if you love her as much as I think you do," Milek said, "I think you know what you have to do."

Let her go...

The words were ringing in his head when he rang the bell at the front of her store. The gate was down yet, covering the door and windows. But she opened up the door, then unlocked and lifted the gate with his help. Metal screeched as it rose high enough for him to duck through the open door with her and Cujo, who stayed by her side. Like Logan wished he could.

Her shop was as vibrant and vivacious as she was—filled with sparkling stones and gleaming metals. Necklaces and earrings and bracelets dangled from displays on the counter. And inside the display cases, smaller pieces glittered and shone, drawing his attention.

"You made all these?" he asked, awed by her talent.

She nodded.

"They're beautiful." One piece in particular piqued his interest. A diamond sparkled between two rubies in a band of braided yellow gold. He would have liked to have slid that ring on her finger someday—when he proposed for real.

But he couldn't give her a ring now. Not when he had to end their engagement.

"That's my favorite," she said, her breath soft on his cheek as she leaned close to him to stare into the display with him.

He wanted to turn his head. He wanted to kiss her. Heck, he wanted to do more than kiss her. He wanted to carry her upstairs to her apartment and make love to her.

But if he touched her again, he wouldn't have the strength to do what needed to be done for her protection. He closed his eyes and held his breath, unable to look at her or breathe in her sweet, flowery scent.

She moved away from him, and the loss of the heat of her closeness chilled him. She shivered, too, as she walked away. "I know why you're here," she said.

"You do?"

Had her brothers warned her?

She nodded. "You're pretty obvious."

Could she see how much he wanted her? How much he needed her?

"I am?"

"You're breaking our engagement," she said.

Then he wasn't obvious at all. But he had to admit, "I think it's for the best."

Her head jerked in a sharp nod. "It's not like it was real anyway."

Pain jabbed his chest—his heart specifically—and he gasped at the intensity of it. It may not have been real to her, but it had felt real to him.

"So it's what you want, too…"

"It was never supposed to be real," she said. "It was just supposed to stop the attempts on your life."

While there hadn't been one since Robert Cooper had killed himself, Logan was certain he was still being followed. Stalked. He couldn't risk her safety until he knew for sure that no one would try to kill him again and, as her brothers had pointed out, maybe inadvertently hit Stacy instead.

But he couldn't say goodbye completely. He couldn't just walk away...with nothing. "That ring in there." He pointed toward the case. "I want to buy that from you."

"It's not for sale," she said.

"Your business must not do that well if you refuse to part with the merchandise," he teased.

She stared wistfully at the ring. "I told you that's my favorite piece."

And that was why he wanted it—to remember her and how much he'd wanted to put that ring on her finger. But having it would probably just prove a painful reminder of what he'd lost. Even if he wasn't still in danger, they wouldn't have a future—if she couldn't forgive him for his part in her father's death. "Never mind then."

Reluctant to leave, he reached down to pet Cujo. The dog flopped onto his side, encouraging Logan to rub his belly, too. He obliged. "You were the best backup I ever had," he said, "you saved my life more than once."

"And mine," Stacy said.

He'd stalled long enough, so Logan headed toward the door. But he hadn't made it very far before she called out, "Wait!"

He tensed, uncertain what he would do if she wanted him to stay. He couldn't put her at risk. But he would never be able to resist her, either.

He heard the jingling of keys as she opened the

display case. Then she was beside him, pressing something into his hand. His skin heated from the tantalizing contact with hers. But before he could grab her hand and hold on to her, she pulled free and stepped away from him. He opened his palm and stared down at the diamond-and-ruby ring.

"I thought it wasn't for sale," he said.

"It's not," she said. "I don't want you to pay me for it. I just want you to have it."

He stared down at it and now the longing was all his. He wanted it, but he wanted it on her finger.

She uttered a shaky chuckle. "I don't know what you're going to do with it. Give it to your mom?"

She wasn't the woman he wanted to wear it. He could only imagine it on one woman's hand. He offered it back. "It's your favorite piece. You should keep it."

She shook her head. "I want you to have it—in appreciation."

"Appreciation?"

"Cujo wasn't the only one who saved my life more than once," she said. "You did, too."

"I was the one who put you in danger," he said. "It was my fault." And that was why he couldn't put that ring on her finger. But he would keep it. He closed his fingers around the metal and stones and headed for the door.

She murmured, "It was easier to hate you."

He turned back to ask her, "Easier than what?"

and he noticed the tears glistening in her smoky-gray eyes. Cujo moved closer to her, as if offering comfort. And as if realizing that it was Logan's fault that she was upset, he uttered a low growl at him.

She shook her head, refusing to answer him.

"Hate me again, then," he said, hoping that hating him would stop her tears. "Remember that it's my fault you lost your father. It was because of my need for justice." He shook his head. "It wasn't justice. You were right. I wanted revenge."

But now the revenge was on him—because he was the one who'd lost everything. And if he didn't find out soon who was after him, he might even lose his life.

Chapter Twenty

It had been so much easier to hate him than to love him like she did. Through the tears stinging her eyes, she could barely see Amber standing on the other side of the display case. She'd immediately called her after Logan left. Her friend's beautiful face was now twisted into a grimace of sympathy. And Stacy began to cry again.

"Why didn't you tell him how you feel about him?" Amber asked. "It's obvious how much you love him."

Stacy shook her head, refusing to admit to feelings that weren't reciprocated. "Ignore this," she said, gesturing toward her wet face. "I'm just on emotional overload. It's been so crazy that I never had the chance to mourn my father."

"So your tears are for him?"

They should have been. He hadn't been the perfect man she'd thought he had been, but he'd been a better man than many had believed. An innocent man. Relatively...

A pang of guilt struck her already aching heart, and she shook her head. "I'm just an emotional mess."

"Are you…"

She tried to focus on her friend again. "What?"

Amber arched a brow. "Could you be…?"

She froze in shock as she realized that her friend thought she could be pregnant. And it dawned on Stacy that she very well could be. They hadn't used protection any time they'd made love.

"You could be," Amber answered her own question. "What will you do if you are?"

She loved Amber, but she wouldn't do what she had. She wouldn't keep her child from his father. "I promised Logan no more secrets."

"So then you've already told him that you love him," Amber said.

And another pang of guilt struck Stacy. She was still keeping one secret from him.

Amber chuckled. "So you've not been entirely honest with him."

Stacy shrugged. "I am not going to tell him that I love him when I know that he doesn't love me."

"Are you sure about that?"

She nodded. "Definitely."

"Because I saw the way he protected you—"

"That's just his job," Stacy said. "That's who he is—a bodyguard. A lawman."

"I think you should tell him how you feel," Amber persisted.

"I haven't always agreed with your decisions, either," Stacy reminded her. "But I've supported you."

Amber sighed. "I hope you don't regret your decision."

Did Amber regret hers?

Before she could ask, the door to the shop opened. Her pulse quickened as she glanced up, hoping it was Logan, hoping that he'd changed his mind and had come back to propose for real.

But it was her brothers.

Amber's face turned a mottled shade of red and she averted her gaze from Milek. But he spared her only a glance. His focus was on Stacy. So was Garek's, his gray eyes dark with concern and fear.

She shuddered. They had never looked at her like that before, not even when she'd told them that their father had died. Her stomach dropped with dread, and she lifted a hand to her mouth to hold back a sob.

"No, no…" Then she forced herself to drag in a deep breath, forced herself to calm down, because she wanted them to tell her the truth. She had to know. "Is he dead? Is Logan dead?"

Amber gasped and grabbed her arm, silently offering her support. But Garek stepped closer and pulled her into his arms. Stacy slammed her hands into his chest, pushing him back.

"Tell me! Tell me!"

"You didn't see the news?" Milek asked.

It played out on a small screen in the corner of the store, but she had muted the volume. She glanced up at it and saw that the news had broken into regular programming. Crews filmed outside a familiar-looking brick building, smoke rising up from an SUV burning at the curb nearly obliterated the sign on the building. But she discerned that the words on the sign spelled out Payne Protection Agency.

The volume was off but the report streamed on the bottom. "Explosion believed to be car bomb. Two confirmed casualties. One injured en route to the hospital."

Two confirmed casualties...

She screamed and clutched at Garek. But then she pushed him back again. "We have to go to the hospital."

"He would have been in the SUV," Garek said. "He would have been one of the dead. The other was probably his twin or his sister..."

She wanted to deny it, but her brother was probably right. "We have to be there," she said. "Mrs. Payne was there for us so many times."

Milek spoke up. "She's right. We need to go."

Garek cupped her face in his hands and stared

down at her, studying her. "Can you handle this?" he asked.

No. If her brothers were right, she had just lost the man she loved. Her worst fears were confirmed at the hospital. The injured man lying in the hospital bed wasn't Logan; he had to have been one of the casualties.

But instead of needing comfort, his mother was offering comfort to some other women in the waiting room, and Garek and Milek had gone to interrogate doctors and nurses for more information. So Stacy walked up to the bed alone, tears streaming down her face as she focused on Logan's twin.

"Is—is he…?"

Parker's face—so handsome and so like Logan's—was scratched and bruised. And his blue eyes were nearly vacant as he stared up at her as if he had no idea who she was. Or who he was…

But she knew: he wasn't Logan. The man she loved was gone.

IT WAS WORSE. So much worse than Logan could have imagined. How on earth had he not put it all together before this—before lives had been lost? Two of his employees had died because they'd jumped into a Payne Protection Agency company SUV and it had been wired to explode.

One of those casualties could have been Stacy. Her brothers ran up to him in the hall. He braced himself, expecting Garek to throw a punch. "You were right," he said. "You were absolutely right about my putting her in danger. I'm glad I listened to you."

He was so grateful that he'd listened to them.

Garek grabbed him as he'd suspected he would. But instead of slugging or shoving him, he pulled him close and...*embraced* him. "Thank God you're all right," his longtime enemy said. "It would have devastated her if you'd died."

His heart clutched. "She's here?"

Milek nodded and then pointed toward his brother's room. "She's in there."

He turned toward the room, but he could see only a shadow through the door. "Does she think Parker is me?"

"No, she thinks you're dead."

Pain at the thought of leaving her clutched his heart. "What? Why?"

"The news reported two casualties," Milek said.

"Damn it!" Logan pushed past Garek and headed toward his brother's room.

Stacy was sitting on his bed, holding his hand. In sickness and health, but what about love? Maybe she did think Parker was him...

But then she turned, as if she felt his presence, and saw him. And she jumped up from the bed and vaulted at him. "You're alive!" She threw her arms around his neck, clutching him close. Tears from her face streaked down his neck and dampened his shirt.

He pulled her back so he could see her face—her beautiful face. Her eyes glistened with more tears. Happy tears.

"I'm sorry," she said. "I'm sorry for crying all over you. But I'm just so happy you're alive."

"Your brother did the same thing when he saw me in the hall," he said. "Got all emotional over me."

"Milek?" She laughed.

"Garek."

She laughed harder. "No!"

"Seems he's kind of sweet on me," he said, and ignored the good-natured curse from the hall. "What about you? Are you sweet on me?"

She drew in a deep breath and then murmured as if to remind herself, "No more secrets."

"You've been keeping one from me?" God, was she pregnant? He'd worried that she might not tell him if she was.

"I'm in love with you," she said, and then she was in his arms again.

But he was the one who'd pulled her close this time. "I thought you hated me again. That you blamed me for causing your father's death," he said. "It was my fault he didn't get parole..."

"Robert Cooper might have had him killed anyway," she said. "You can't blame yourself for that

I don't." She pulled back to look at his face again. "Is that why you broke our engagement?"

"I didn't want to," he confessed. "But I didn't want you in danger." He forced himself to release her and to step back. "I didn't want to lose you forever the way we've lost two employees. Like we nearly lost Parker."

His twin groaned. "I'm coming back. Damn explosion addled my brain."

Logan didn't know what *his* excuse was. While he'd been in his office when the bomb went off, his walls had only shook a little. But maybe it had shaken him up enough to come to his senses and put it all together.

"The bomb was in your SUV," he told his twin. Their employees had unfortunately asked to borrow it for a fast-food run. "And the bomb was in your house…"

Stacy's eyes widened as she realized what he had when he'd rushed outside to find Parker's SUV burning. "Whoever was trying to kill you wasn't trying to kill *you*," she said. "He was trying to kill Parker."

"I'm still in danger, though," he said, "because someone keeps mistaking me for him. And me being in danger puts you in danger, too."

"I have a thought about that," Parker said, and as he sat up, he nearly toppled out of the bed.

Logan's heart clutched with concern for his

brother. "You're lucky you can think at all with that concussion." But the doctors had already assured them that it wasn't life threatening.

"It's nothing," he said. And compared to what had happened to two of their employees, it was. "I can handle it. And I can handle whoever's after me. Take your fiancée and elope. Get the hell out of here."

Logan shook his head. "I can't leave you alone—not to face this kind of danger."

"You just said you don't want to lose her," Parker argued. "So don't put her in danger."

"We can help," Garek Kozminski offered as he stepped into the room with Milek. "We want to help."

"What are you saying?" Logan asked. "You want me to hire you?"

Garek outright laughed but then he shrugged. "I don't know. Maybe you should. It took me just a couple of calls to learn what you guys have yet to figure out."

"What?"

"Someone put out a hit on Parker Payne."

Logan stared at him in shock. That explained all the different attempts on their lives—different assassins. It was much worse than he'd thought.

Garek continued, "I'm sorry, man, sorry that I thought it was you putting our sister in danger

I shouldn't have interfered. I can see that you love her."

"Do you?" she asked hopefully.

How did she not know?

Because he was an idiot...

He dropped to his knees and pulled out the ring she'd given him—her favorite piece. "I love you with all my heart, Stacy Kozminski. Will you marry me, really marry me? Will you become my wife—my partner—for the rest of our lives?"

She nodded. "Yes, of course, I'll marry you." She held her hand steady as he slid the ring on to her finger.

"And we'll all work together to make sure those lives are very long," Garek assured them.

Penny Payne clapped her hands together, drawing their attention to where she stood in the doorway. "See, I told you they're good boys."

Logan laughed. "I don't know about that," he said. "But they're family now." Just like the Paynes, the Kozminskis protected the ones they loved. With their help, he believed they could keep Stacy and Parker safe.

"One big dysfunctional family," Garek added.

Her gesture was small, just her palm sliding over her stomach, but Logan caught it. And hope burgeoned inside him like a baby might be burgeoning inside his fiancée.

Their family was probably going to be getting

even bigger. But first they had to make certain that they didn't lose one. That no one carried out that hit on his twin.

"Together we can handle anything," Stacy declared, as if she sensed his concern. "My father was right. You are the man for me."

"And you're the woman for me." He hoped his mother still had her connection to rush the marriage license. He didn't want to wait another moment before making Stacy his bride.

He had no doubt their lives would be full of danger and craziness, but, more than that, it would be full of love.

* * * * *